BATTERED

BATTERED

ANDREA CRIST HECKNER

This book is dedicated to all of us who were/are told what our limits are. Pursue your dreams with all your heart. Never let others small minded views limit you.

Contents

Trigger Warning

TRIGGER WARNING

Potential Spoilers Below

This book includes Domestic Violence and Murder.
Reader Discretion is Advised.

> *If you or someone you know is experiencing domestic violence, help is available:*
> *The National Domestic Violence Hotline*
> *1-800-799-7233*

BOOK 5

SECRETS IN THE HEARTLAND SERIES

ANDREA CRIST HECKNER

1

Chained

February 4, 2024
Lindsey

Chained in the basement again. That is my first thought as I float back to consciousness. *At least I know what set Mack off this time* was my second. Slowly rising, I assess my injuries by sight, touch, and level of pain. Busted lip, swollen, bruised eye, bruises all over my torso and probably a broken rib, those were the first injuries that I cataloged. Despite all that, it was worth it as long as Claire got my note. It's already worth this beating and the time I will spend down here chained in the cold, dim, damp basement because for the first time in a long time I have hope.

I sit back down and let my mind wander. When Mack asked me to move to Denver with him, I thought it was going to be the perfect new beginning for the two of us, and at first it was. We sold my car before we moved to pay the deposit and first month's rent on the house we live in. Mack said that we would share his truck until we saved up enough to buy me another vehicle. Plus, Denver has a phenomenal public transportation system, so I could get anywhere I needed to go.

Mack went right to work for his cousin's marijuana dispensary and I spent those first few weeks making our house a home.

When we lived in Springfield, I worked for a big box store for five years, so it was easy to transfer to the location closest to our house. I was working second shift, since that was Mack's schedule as well. He would drop me off and pick me up from work most of the time and we got to spend a lot of time together, but I was lonely. I missed my best friend, Claire, and my parents, but they hated Mack, and I basically had to choose between them and him. I know now that I made the wrong choice, but I had really believed that Mack loved me and wanted it to work between us. I started making friends with some people I worked with. That was my next mistake. Talking to people at work.

Mack was watching me, testing me, and when I let one of my co-workers, a guy named Lee, buy me lunch when I had no money or food, it set Mack off. He sent me a text that night, telling me he was working late and that I should take the bus home. It had happened before, so I thought nothing of it until I got home and saw Mack's truck in the driveway. The only things that I remember Mack saying were "Whore and Slut" as he beat me to unconsciousness. That was the first time I woke up, chained in the basement, but obviously not the last.

2

The Note

Friday March 1, 2024
Claire

Like most people nowadays, almost all the mail that I get is junk, which has led me to pile it up to go through on my day off. Sitting at the kitchen table drinking coffee, I start sorting the almost three weeks' worth of mail. The recycling bin sits right next to me on the floor, so I start just chucking things into it without even bothering to open them. I throw the nondescript white envelope in the bin on the top of the pile, but pause and look at it again. Something about the handwriting of my name and address is eerily familiar. The envelope has no return address and had been machine stamped, which had initially led me to believe it was junk.

I pick the envelope up out of the recycling can and slit it open. A small torn off piece of paper flutters onto the table. Picking it up, I see that written on one side is Large Pineapple Anchovy Pizza, when I turn it over and there's an address in Denver, Colorado. The paper slips from my fingers back onto the table. Large Pineapple Anchovy

Pizza is the code phrase that Lindsey and I have used since we were young girls. My mom had come up with the code so that we would know if someone was safe for us to go with if there was ever an emergency. Later, when we were teenagers, we agreed to keep using the phrase, if either of us needed help or felt unsafe. One time at a party in high school, I whispered to Lindsey, "I'm hungry, let's go get a large pineapple anchovy pizza", she grabbed my hand, and we left immediately. I remember telling her as we drove home that I saw some guys pouring something into the punch and felt like we had to get out of there.

It has been almost two years since any of us have heard from Lindsey, and now I know for sure that my best friend is in trouble. The post mark on the envelope is from over three weeks ago. The question in my mind now is: *Should I tell the Petersons or head to Denver on my own?* This is yet another time when I wish I could ask my mom what to do. None of the tapes she left me covered when your best friend is in serious trouble and she reaches out to you.

3

Lonesome Highway

Saturday March 2, 2024

Claire

It is always disorienting for me to wake up in a place I have never slept before, but after a few moments, my brain kicks in. I am in Salina, Kansas, at a hotel just off I-70. I drove as far as I could yesterday once I decided to head to Denver on my own. I'm not sure what I am going to find in Denver and I don't want to get the Peterson's hopes up. As crime scene technicians for the Springfield Police Department, we work on rotating schedules and my team built up a lot of comp. time on the last case. So, I am off for two more days but I could put in for more time off if I need it. Hopefully, I will find Lindsey right away and get her to come with me, then we can start the drive back.

After grabbing the complimentary breakfast at the hotel and a quick stop for gas, I am ready to continue to drive. Driving my mom's Buick Encore with its rebuilt engine and transmission gives me a sense of connection to her. My dad has been trying to convince me to buy a new car, but I plan to drive this one until the wheels fall off. With my dad's wife, Dawn, servicing it, that may never happen. I'm almost in Denver when my phone rings, it's my dad.

"Hi, Dad. What's up?"

"Hi Sweetie. Dawn and I just stopped by your place because I thought you were off work for the next few days and we wanted to see if you wanted to grab a late lunch."

"Normally, I would love to, but I am actually on my way to Colorado. I am headed to pick up Lindsey and bring her home."

"Oh, I didn't realize that she had reached out to you. Are you alone?"

"Yeah, why? Who else would be with me?"

"I just meant that I just worry about that Mack guy. Please be careful."

"I will. I have to go because traffic is getting heavy and I need to pay attention to the GPS. Love you. Say Hi to Dawn for me."

"Okay, one more question, then I will let you go. Do you have the credit card that I gave you?"

"Yes, dad I have it but I can pay for this trip myself."

"Yeah, I know you can, but don't hesitate to use that card if you need to."

"Alright, I will use it if I need it."

"Bye, call me tonight. Please. Love you."

"Yes, dad I will call you tonight. Love you."

I sigh after I make sure my phone is hung up. My dad can be so hovering and over protective sometimes. *What would mom think if she could see the way he is now?* I wonder as I merge into the lane to take the exit my GPS told me to. Before my mom was kidnapped and murdered, my relationship with my dad was nonexistent, but since losing her, he has become a big part of my life.

Once I am off the interstate, I notice that it is not the nicest neighborhood. The houses are not being well cared for with overgrown lawns and chipping paint. There is stray garbage on the streets and at least one dismantled car in someone's lawn. I follow the GPS computer voice as she guides me into more and more rundown areas. There is a payday loan store on one side of the corner and a bar on the other, with a bunch of guys hanging out in front of it. A lot of the houses have bars on their windows and fences around their front yards. I make the last turn and look ahead as it quips that the location is on the left. I pull up to the curb at the house just before it. I am not sure if Mack would recognize my SUV, but I at least need to be a little careful. I sit there wondering what to do next. I realize that I didn't plan this out and have no way to let Lindsey know I am here other than to walk up to the door and knock.

I take a deep breath, send up a prayer to my mom, open the door, and step out into the crisp, mountain air. A woman who appears to be in her seventies is moving as quickly as she can towards me. I have no idea who she is and I am about to start walking when she calls out, "Claire?"

"Yes, I am Claire, but do I know you?"

"No, but I know Lindsey, and you can't just walk up to her place. He is still home. Please come into my house and I will tell you what I know."

I nod and follow her up the stairs into the house I parked in front of. The exterior of the house is likely the best maintained one in the neighborhood. As we walk inside, I see the interior is tidy and well kept. The woman shows me into her kitchen and motions for me to sit.

She is standing at the stove, starting a kettle of water, when she says, "I'm Emma Jean Harris, by the way. I will tell you what I know about Lindsey and that asshole she lives with. I have lived in this house since I was a new bride of just eighteen years old. This was a great community when we moved in, we raised our kids here and I have watched it slowly fall apart. But that isn't why you are here. If I have this right, you are here to save Lindsey."

"Save Lindsey from what?"

"Not what, honey. Who? And the answer to that is Mack. I have been around long enough to know a wife beater when I see one."

"How do you know who I am?"

"At the beginning of February, I was outside picking up before the trash truck came when Lindsey walked out to the curb with a bag. I hadn't seen her in a long time, like almost a year, and she looked rough. I went over, hugged her, and she slipped something in my hand and whispered, 'Don't look at this until you are inside.'. Then she turned, put the garbage bag in their can and went back inside. She gave me an envelope with your name and address on the front. I know it's wrong to look at other people's mail so I didn't open it. I wrote your name and address down in case I ever needed it, then drove to the post office and mailed the envelope to you. That envelope is why you are here, right?"

"Yes, but I don't know what to do now that I am here."

"I have some ideas." Emma Jean stated, and then she began to laugh.

4

Losing Hope

Saturday March 2, 2024

Lindsey

I'm sitting in the kitchen drinking black coffee when Mack stumbles down the stairs. It's two in the afternoon but I learned a long time ago not to comment on his habits. He opens the fridge, grabs an energy drink and slams the door. The only things in there are his energy drinks, diet soda and salad mix. Mack eats when he is at work or out with his friends, getting high. He buys all the groceries we have and brings me only food with little or no calories. I am at my lowest weight ever and have very little energy, but Mack is happy with the way I look, so at least that is something.

When he let me out of the basement after the last incident, the only thing he said to me was that I knew better than to leave the house. I thought about defending myself by telling him that all I did was take a bag of trash to the curb, but he knew what happened since he watches me on the cameras. Trying to plead with him that I did nothing wrong would just serve to make him angry again, so I had just nodded. There was no way he saw me hand the envelope to our neighbor, Mrs. Harris, when she hugged me. Because if he had, there would have been an interrogation and I might not be alive today. Mack added new locks to the doors that required a key to open on both sides. I sent that note to Claire when I realized that Mack was going to kill me at some point. I don't want to die.

I have started to lose hope that Claire got my note, or maybe she hadn't understood it. It's been almost a month, and I hoped that she would have come to help me escape by now. There is no way I am getting out of here on my own. Mack keeps my only pair of shoes in his truck and I have no money, phone or friends. I understand now that us moving to Colorado was a way for him to have complete control over me. The isolation and complete dependence on Mack makes me feel like a child, but somewhere deep inside of me screams a voice of a woman who wants to be set free. I never understood why women stayed in abusive relationships until I found myself trapped in this one.

Mack looks me over, sneers, then turns and walks out of the house, locking it behind him. One of his rules is that I am not to speak unless spoken to. I am okay with this rule because I never know what will set him off, so not speaking is safe. I watch out the kitchen window as Mack backs his truck out of the garage, down the driveway, then turns and drives down the street. A sense of momentary peace settles over me, with him out of the house I am safe. At least for now.

I stand up and watch him pull out of the driveway. I drop the curtain when I see Emma Jean at her window. I have a black eye and a busted lip and I don't want her to see that. She is the sweetest person I have ever met. When Mack and I first moved in, she welcomed us to the neighborhood and used to leave baked goods on the front porch for us. I am pretty sure Mack scared her off because one day, the treats just stopped coming. I shudder to think what she must think of me and what is going on in this house.

As exhausted as I am, I can't go lay down yet for two reasons. First, Mack sometimes comes back after a short time instead of being gone to work for hours. The second is that I need to run on the treadmill for at least an hour. Mack checks the treadmills log every time he comes home and I know if I haven't exercised, that it will set him off. So, despite only having eaten two apples in the last twenty-four hours and only having a pair of slipper socks on, I will run. While I am running, I remind myself over and over that maybe one day all this running will save my life. I dream of running from Mack, but I just haven't been able to yet.

5

The Plan

Saturday March 2, 2024

Claire

I sit at Emma Jean's kitchen table drinking tea and waiting for her to tell me her plan. She hasn't spoken since she told me she had ideas instead busily preparing a roast to go into the oven. She stops and points out the kitchen window.

"There goes that jerk. He should be gone the rest of the night. He might be back around midnight, but often it isn't until the morning."

I stand up and join Emma Jean at the window. I glimpse the beat up, black F150 as it drives down the street in the opposite direction of Emma Jean's house. It is the same truck that Mack drove when he and Lindsey lived in Springfield. I see a flutter across the way as the curtain settles back over the window. I wonder if that is Lindsey.

"Okay, Mrs. Harris, what now?"

"Now we wait awhile and make sure he isn't coming back."

The back door opens and shuts as she says this and a man calls out, "Darling, who is that parked in front of our house with the Missouri license plates?"

13

A man who seems very fit and virile for his age steps into view. He looks from me to Emma Jean and then back to me again.

"Sorry, I didn't know EJ was entertaining company. I don't believe we have met. I am Marlin Harris and you are?"

"Hello, sir. I'm Claire Learner and that's my SUV in front of your house."

"None of that sir business just call me Marlin or Harris. How do you know EJ?"

The confusion must be clear on my face because Emma Jean interjects, "This is my husband Marlin, and he's the one and only person on the planet who calls me EJ. Marlin, sweetheart, this is the Claire that I mailed that letter from Lindsey to."

Understanding becomes apparent in Marlin's expression as he sits down across from me. Emma Jean sets a cup of coffee in front of him with no prompting and he reaches up and squeezes her hand. "Thank you, dear. Alrighty, Claire, now that you have arrived, please tell us what was in that envelope and what your plan is to help Lindsey?"

"Well, I can answer one of those questions. The envelope had a note from Lindsey asking for me to come and help her. As for a plan, I don't have one, but Emma Jean told me she does."

"Really, what is her plan?"

"She hasn't shared it with me yet."

Marlin and Emma Jean both begin to laugh. As their laughter dissipates, Emma Jean says, "Okay, I will tell you both what I think we should do. Marlin, you will need to indulge me a bit as I need to tell Claire some background information that you already know. Then I will lay out how I think we get Lindsey out of that house and away from the asshole."

Marlin smiles, turns to me, "Claire, you should know that the only time I hear my dear EJ swear is when she talks about Mack. She has developed a genuine hatred for the man. I do, of course, understand why she feels the way she does, but it is still a bit of a shock to hear her use curse words."

Emma Jean is leveling him with a stare. "Marlin, a long time ago you told me that sometimes the only word that completely covers a situation or person is a curse word. If it was good enough for you, it is certainly good enough for me."

As much as part of me is enjoying the give and take of this couple's verbal banter and witnessing how much they love each other despite all the years they have been together, I wish Emma Jean would just tell me her plan.

"Claire, please bear with me as I tell you some things about Marlin. When I tell you my plan, it will become clear why you needed to know about my dear husband."

"That's fine. Please go on."

"When I met Marlin, I was sixteen, and he was twenty. It was nineteen sixty-four and the United States was on the brink of entering the Vietnam War. Marlin had just finished training to be a Marine and was home on leave. We both went to a USO dance and when I saw him, it was love at first sight for me."

Marlin reaches over and takes a hold of Emma Jean's hand again. He raises it to his mouth, kisses it and says, "For me too!"

She smiles at him and continues, "We saw each other every day for two weeks and then Marlin had to report back to Camp Pendleton. That is when our letter writing started and continued for two years while he was fighting in Vietnam. When Marlin finally returned home, he proposed, and we were married. He became a police officer here in Denver, and I stayed home and raised our boys.

I already told you that we moved into this house right after we got married and have lived here for the last fifty-plus years. The Shermans were our next-door neighbors for forty-five of those years. We played cards, had barbecues, and raised our families together. I tell you this because both Marlin and I have been in that house hundreds of times and know that it is laid out just like ours. When Alvin Sherman died five years ago, their daughters convinced Georgiana to move near them in Colorado Springs. The one thing that Georgiana would not give in to was selling the house. That is how it became a rental. The first people to move in were a nice family who were new to town. They lived there for almost three years until they bought a house. That is when Lindsey and Mack moved in.

At first, Marlin and I thought they were a nice young couple. I brought cookies over the day after they moved in, and Lindsey was friendly and welcoming. For the first six months they were here, they both waved and said hi each time I saw them. Then Lindsey stopped going to work, and Mack just nodded when we saw him. Marlin is the one who pointed out all the security cameras that were installed. I didn't know what to think, but as time went on, we rarely saw Lindsey—and when we did, she looked skinnier and skinnier, and rougher and rougher. I put two and two together. Mack was abusing her.

Marlin was retired from the police force by then, but he knew plenty of guys on the job still. He had a couple of them stop in and do a welfare check. Lindsey denied that anything was wrong. There was nothing else they could do. Which left Marlin and me with nothing to do but watch and wait. Ever since Lindsey slipped me that letter, I have prayed you were coming to help her and now here you are."

Emma Jean picks up her teacup and takes a long drink while I try to figure out how Lindsey ended up in this situation.

"There is one more thing about Marlin, I need to tell you before laying out the plan. My dear husband is a big-time prankster and loves practical jokes. He found a kindred soul in Alvin Sherman, so the two of them kept Georgiana and I on our toes for many years. One of their favorite tricks was to flip the main breaker in the outside breaker box and turn the power off to each other's house."

Marlin starts laughing and adds, "Yeah, that one used to make both of you furious, but it was hilarious."

Emma Jean once again levels him with her stare and then continues, "Marlin, you and I can argue about that once Lindsey and Claire are safely on their way out of Denver. Claire, my idea stems from that joke. Because of the security cameras, we know that Mack is watching everything that goes on over there. So, we are going to turn the power off to the house, then you are going over there to get Lindsey. I figure we have ten or fifteen minutes until Mack could get back home once he notices the cameras are off."

Marlin smiles and says, "Why EJ, that might just work. The one thing that concerns me is that he may see us turn the power off. We don't know what angles those cameras cover, so we can't plan for how to evade them."

Now that I know Emma Jean's plan, it is my turn to talk. "I think I should be the one to turn it off. Mack is going to know that it is me anyway, because Lindsey has no one else to turn to. Also, that way, he won't have any reason to think you two are involved. So, Marlin, explain to me how to shut off the power."

6

Escape

Saturday March 2, 2024
Claire

Mack has been gone for over an hour now, and during that time, Marlin and Emma Jean have shown me where the main breaker is on their house and how to turn it off. Marlin handed me a bolt cutter as the breaker on Mack and Lindsey's place has a padlock on it. The plan is that Emma Jean and Marlin will sit on their front porch drinking glasses of lemonade, looking to all the world to be a sweet, retired couple enjoying the late afternoon breeze. Really, they are serving as my lookouts and will alert me if Mack or anyone else approaches the house. Marlin has an air horn that was left over from a recent race that he volunteered at and is ready to use it.

I hug both of them while we are still in the kitchen, there will be no time for goodbyes after I have Lindsey out of that house. They head towards the front door and their porch as I head out the back door towards the house Lindsey is in. My heart is beating so fast that I have to stop at the bottom of the three steps and take a few calming breaths. When Lindsey and I were teenagers, we used to swear that we would die for one another. I love her like she is my biological sister, and this is the moment that I will prove that indeed I will put my life at risk to save hers.

I walk straight to the breaker and put the shackle of the lock between the blades of the bolt cutter. I squeeze with all my might, using both my hands, and in about twenty seconds, it works. I swing open the breaker box and pull down the lever. There is a slight humming but nothing else noticeable, so I run towards the back door and start pounding while shouting.

"Lindsey, it is Claire! Open this door or I am going to break in! "

I immediately hear running and then see the face of my best friend as she pulls back the curtain. I gasp in shock; she is battered and looks like a skeleton of the person I have known most of my life.

"Oh my God, you are here. Thank you. My prayers have been answered."

Lindsey is crying, but she hasn't opened the door.

"You need to open the door so I can get you out of there."

"I can't. Ever since I mailed that letter to you, Mack locks all the doors with keys and he takes them with him when he leaves."

Looking down, I see the bolt cutters I'm holding in my hand, and I raise them up. "Stand back. I am going to break the window out of this door."

Watching as Lindsey backs almost all the way out of the kitchen, I smash the window with all my might. It shatters! "Lindsey, go put your shoes on and grab towels, pillows, whatever, so you can climb through this window without getting hurt."

She nods and runs off. While she is gone, I break out all the shards of glass that I can. A few minutes later she comes back, arms loaded with bedding and wearing what appears to be a pair of men's hiking boots. She pushes a chair to the window and we work together to put all the bedding across the window frame. At last Lindsey climbs out into my arms. I hug her tight and she hugs back even tighter.

"We need to leave now." Lindsey says in a frantic voice. "He is watching."

"I agree, but didn't you notice the house had no power, so he isn't able to watch us right now."

"No, he is watching. I figured he didn't pay the power bill again, but I know from when that has happened before that his cameras work, even when the house has no power."

"Then we better run!"

We take off running and I am surprised by how fast Lindsey is despite looking so frail. I throw the bolt cutters behind my SUV, just like Marlin told me to. Both of them are watching us from their porch and I see Emma Jean wink at me as we pull away from the curb. Lindsey is shaking in the passenger seat. I almost ask if she is okay, but I know the answer to that question, so I just drive. I want to put as much distance between us and Denver as I can before we stop for the night.

Two and a half hours later, I pull over to get gas. I call my dad as I pump gas, relieved that he doesn't answer so I can just leave a voicemail.

"Hi Dad, Lindsey and I are on our way back home. She is in rough shape, so it is probably best if I don't talk to you in front of her. I will call you again as soon as I can. Love you."

Hopefully, my message will reassure him enough to not call back because I don't know what I would say to him. My best friend looks like she has been a prisoner of war and for all intents and purposes, I broke her out of jail. She is convinced that her maniac, hopefully ex-boyfriend, is chasing us and we have nine more hours to drive. I have no desire to tell my dad any of those things over the phone. When we get closer to Springfield, I am going to call the Petersons and have them meet us at my house.

After pumping gas, I used the bathroom and wandered around the convenience store. I bought two diet sodas, an apple, some turkey snack sticks, a bag of chips, three candy bars, an energy drink, and a t-shirt for Lindsey. The shirt says 'Colorado Blows' on it with a picture of a joint. I hope the shirt will make her laugh. Just like when I got to Denver, I don't really have a plan, but hopefully, while we drive, we can figure out together what to do next.

My SUV is locked when I get back to it and Lindsey is laying down in her seat. I left the keys in the ignition, so I knock on the window. She jumps up in her seat, startled, and puts her arms over her face and head. She peers out at me through the crook of one of her arms, then hits the button to unlock the doors.

7

Going Home

Saturday March 2, 2024
Lindsey

I know this is a dream. I must have fallen asleep or passed out on the floor of the living room after running. There is no way I am in Claire's SUV, driving away from my nightmare. Claire hasn't said a thing since she practically squealed away from the curb in front of my neighbor's house. It has been a long time since I have had such a vivid dream. I jolt awake and try to get up, but something stops me. I'm about to scream when I hear Claire's voice next to me.

"Lindsey...Lindsey...Lindsey!"

I realize that I really am in Claire's SUV and that it is a seatbelt that stopped me from getting up. I turn my head and see my best friend. This is real, Claire saved me. I begin to cry. Silently! Letting the tears stream down my face.

"Lindsey, what's wrong? How can I help?" Claire says as she reaches across the center console and places her hand on mine.

I smile, although not big. This is too good to be true. "Wrong? Nothing is wrong. You actually came and got me out. Thank you so much, but why are we stopping? Mack will be on our trail and we need to get out of Colorado as fast as possible."

"I love you, Lindsey, and there is nothing I wouldn't do for you. We have been on the road for over two hours and I have to get gas. Do you want to go in the store with me, or do you want me to get you anything?"

I look down at myself. I'm wearing Mack's hiking boots, a pair of bike shorts and a sports bra. There are scars and bruises visible all over my body. I don't want to go in and have people gawk at me. "Will you grab me a diet soda and an apple, please?"

Claire looks at me for a few seconds before she responds, "Are you sure that is all you want? I have my dad's credit card, so don't worry about the cost."

She doesn't understand that I have been existing on black coffee, diet soda, apples, dry lettuce mix and grilled chicken breast for the past six months. I don't think my stomach can handle anything else.

"No, just the apple and soda. Thanks."

Claire nods and gets out of the SUV. I watch her pump gas while talking on the phone, but I can't hear who she's talking to. As she walks towards the convenience store. I lock the doors of the SUV and lay my seat down. I don't want to be seen or taken by surprise.

I have no way to begin to talk to Claire about Mack or what I have lived through, so I am relieved when she gets back behind the wheel and starts up an audiobook. I had forgotten how much my friend loves to listen to smutty romance novels while she drives. I'm not sure how far into the book we are, but it doesn't matter because I can't pay attention to it. I keep my eyes on the rearview and passenger side mirrors; watching for any sign of Mack.

I know he is looking for me. He promised me many times that the only way I was ever leaving him was in a body bag. Some people might think this was an idle threat or a turn of phrase, but I know having survived his abuse that he meant it literally. When he finds me, he will kill me and probably Claire too!

As happy as I am that my friend has saved me, I am realizing the very real danger that I have put us both in.

8

Rocky Mountain High

Saturday March 2, 2024

Mack

The store has been slammed tonight. Friday and Saturday nights are always our busiest. My cousin Rocky started this store in two thousand twelve just after recreational marijuana sales became legal here in Colorado. He loves to brag about how he used the money he got from his dad's life insurance to open this place. The best part to Rocky and almost everyone he tells the story to is how anti-drug his dad had been. Rocky and his dad had butted heads his whole life and being able to stick it to his dad one last time by being a successful, legal drug dealer makes Rocky practically giddy.

I love working here. The customers and other employees are chill, Rocky pays me a great wage and commission on the sales I make and, of course, the free product adds to my job satisfaction. The only thing that I hate about this job is Rocky's ban on personal electronic devices in the store. As soon as I get to work, I have to turn my phone off and put it in a Faraday lockbox. He even makes customers leave their cell phones behind when they come into the store. It wouldn't matter if you snuck a device in, he has the best signal jamming equipment money can buy. Rocky is paranoid that the federal government listens to people through their phones and that cannabis businesses are a major target of the DEA.

Moving to Colorado is the best decision I have ever made. I'm finally out from under the shadow of my dad and oldest brother. Being a Tiswell back home in Springfield meant that everyone expected me to be a criminal, or at the very least, a screwup. But that simply isn't true here. Rocky is my cousin on my mom's side, so a totally different last name. His mom, my aunt Stacey, has told me that my mom marrying my dad broke their parents' hearts. Seems no one on my mom's side of the family could ever stand my dad. Living in Denver has been great, and not just because I can legally smoke all the pot I want. Although that is a part of it. I go out with the people from work almost every night and there are some hot chicks that party with our group. Lindsey is always home waiting for me, but I'm too young to be with just one girl. I keep it casual with the party girls and figure what Lindsey doesn't know doesn't hurt her. My only gripes have to do with Lindsey. She knows all my buttons and even after correction continues to push them, although it is getting to be less and less often. Hopefully that means she is settling into our life together and my expectations.

By the time there is a lull in customers, I have been at work almost five hours. I grab my phone and walk over to the local taco joint. My phone starts going crazy just as I pull open the restaurant's door. *What the Hell!* I think as I sit down to look through all the notifications. The power at the house is out and has been for five hours. I must have forgotten to pay the power bill again. I dismiss those notifications and open the camera app. The first motion outside that it captured was a little after three this afternoon. I am livid as I watch that bitch Claire walk up to my backdoor, proceed to break a window and pull Lindsey through it. The two of them then take off running.

I am already on my feet and back over to the store's parking lot before Rocky even answers his phone.

"What's up, cuz?"

"I have to leave and the store has been slammed tonight so you need to come back or some shit,"

"What do you mean, you have to leave? You work for me, stoner, not the other way around."

Rocky isn't wrong, but I am so pissed off right now that I'm not having this conversation. "It's a damn emergency. I will tell you about it later," I say and end the call.

I'm sure that those two dimwits are headed straight back to Springfield, so that is the way I am headed. The biggest issue is they have a five-hour head start on me, but that is fine because it will be better if I have time to plan how to take care of this betrayal. I turn around and head back to the house. I need to gather my stuff and make a plan because I know that Claire is behind this. Lindsey would never leave me on her own.

Lindsey knows her place and that she and I are meant to be together forever. She left me one time when we lived in Springfield and Claire was behind that betrayal as well. Claire and Lindsey's meddling parents, especially her dad, were why I knew that I had to get Lindsey away from Springfield. We have been doing well since we moved to Colorado. Yes, there have been bumps in the road and times I have had to remind Lindsey about the expectations, but all couples go through that.

There will be hell to pay for this little running act and this time Lindsey won't be the only one to pay the price.

9

Irony

Saturday March 2, 2024
Lindsey

It is dark the next time I wake up and I realize that Claire is pulling into a hotel parking lot. I am afraid to stop but also know that I'm in no shape to drive, so I don't say anything.

Claire looks over at me and says, "I have to stop and sleep for a while. I can't keep my eyes open any longer."

"Okay. Where are we?"

"Hays, Kansas. About six hours from home. It is just after eight o'clock, but I have been driving most of the day and need a break. I will go get us a room and be right back."

I watch as my best friend and now savior walks across the parking lot and into the lobby. As far as I know, Mack has no way of tracking me or us, but I wouldn't put anything past him. He has to be on our trail by now, and I don't think that Claire realizes how much danger we're in.

There is something eerily familiar to me about this hotel parking lot. It takes me only a few minutes to realize that Mack and I stayed here on our way to Colorado. That was back when I believed we were headed to our fresh start at happily ever after. Is it irony or fate that Claire would pick this exact hotel to stop at?

I think back to that trip to Colorado with Mack. We sang along to the radio, ate junk food and laughed. Mack was attentive and loving and I never once on that trip questioned if I had made the right choice. I was sure that Mack would propose soon and that when I told my parents and Claire that we are getting married, they would see that they had been wrong about him.

It has been less than ten minutes when I see Claire walking back to the SUV. She has a packet that contains room keys in her hand and smiles as she peers at me through the windshield. It has been a very long time since I have had any sense of optimism or positivity, so her smile is on the verge of annoying me. I know in my head that Claire has been through a tough time with her mom's disappearance and murder, but I still don't think she understands just how hard life really can be.

Claire gets in and drives the SUV to the back of the hotel right by a door. Before getting out, she hands me one of the electronic key cards and says, "I got us the room right next to this door. I thought that would be the best. You know, just in case."

Nodding, I reply, "Thanks. I'm not sure what will keep us safe, because I know Mack will never stop until he gets me back. Even if that means I am dead. What scares me more is I don't think he would hesitate to kill you or anyone else to get to me."

"We won't stay all night. I just need to get some sleep. Let's get you settled in the room, then I will walk across the parking lot to the store. I will get us food and some clothes and shoes for you. How does that sound?"

I find myself nodding again as we walk into the hotel. Claire leaves after a few minutes, and I lock the door behind her. Walking into the bathroom, I lock that door too, then turn off the light, climb into the bathtub and pull the curtain closed. I stand against the wall of the bathtub listening for any sounds. Claire and I agreed she would knock in a one, two, three pattern when she gets back. So, when I hear that series of knocks, I shouldn't hesitate, but I do. Mack has been out-smarting me for so long that I have to wonder if it is him. Then I hear Claire call out, "I have a delivery of a large pineapple and anchovy pizza". She is definitely smarter than me.

Friends and Fear

Saturday March 2, 2024
Claire

I stand in the hall holding the bags from the store, waiting for Lindsey to answer the door. It doesn't surprise me that the knocks weren't enough, but hopefully the pizza comment is because I don't know what to try next. That's when I hear the inside lock being undone and then the door eases open. I follow Lindsey into the room and set the bags down on the desk.

"I got you some leggings, t-shirts, underwear, socks and shoes. I guessed the size for the clothes, but figured your shoe size was the same." I am pulling the items out of the bag and handing them to Lindsey as I talk.

"You didn't have to get all this, but thank you."

"Well, I did make you leave without packing anything, so I figured all your stuff will have to be replaced."

"It isn't like I have a lot. Mack keeps my shoes in his truck, and I only have sports bras and shorts for clothes. He got rid of all my other stuff, so really, I didn't need to pack."

"Well then, that settles that. You needed clothes and shoes and I got you some. I also got you a phone. It is a prepaid one, so I got you a minutes card, too."

"You really didn't need to do that."

"Yes, I did because we will both feel safer if you have a way to get a hold of me and vice versa. When we get back home and you get a job or whatever, you can get a real cell phone, but until then you and I are the ones that know you have this and its phone number."

"You will never know how much I appreciate you." Lindsey says and begins to sob.

All I wanted to do was help my friend but watching her body rack with sobs I feel utterly helpless. I finish taking the things I bought out of the bags. I set Lindsey's favorite snacks from when we lived together next to the bag of apples, then pulled out the two frozen low-calorie dinners I got us for tonight.

"Do you want the crustless chicken pot pie or the enchilada meal?"

Lindsey looks up at me and shrugs, "Whichever one you don't want will be fine with me."

"Well, I only bought the ones we both used to eat, but the enchilada sounds better to me right now."

After microwaving both meals, we eat in silence. I notice that Lindsey is only picking out the chicken and vegetables from the meal. There is so much I want to ask Lindsey, but I don't think she is ready to talk to me. "I'm going to try to get a few hours of sleep, then we'll finish the drive home. Is that okay with you?"

"Sure." Lindsey says in a small, sad voice as I turn off the light next to my bed and climb under the covers. The light clicks back on and I hear Lindsey say in that same small, defeated voice, "Is it okay if we leave the light on?"

I look at my friend and see the fear on her face. The fear of the dark is definitely a new phobia for Lindsey. She was always the one dragging me to haunted houses and moonlight trail walks. "Yeah, that's fine" is all I can manage before rolling over. I don't want Lindsey to know that I am crying. No one wants anyone to feel sorry for them, but I can't stop the tears or the recurring thoughts that Mack broke Lindsey, and I don't know how to put her back together.

11

Secrets

Saturday March 2, 2024
Mack

When I first got back to the house, I thought that I needed to get on the road as quickly as possible but as I calmed down; I realized I needed to be sure the house was ready for when Lindsey and I returned. I checked the app for the power company on my way back here and my bill is up to date, so I need to find out what Claire did to the power. I rewatch the footage of Claire walking up to the back door and realize that she came from the side of the house. Walking over there, I see the lock for the electrical box laying on the grass. It has clearly been cut off and the box itself is sitting open. The switch is flipped to off. Claire must have thought that if she turned off the power, the cameras would stop working. I say to no one in particular, "No sweetheart, my system is much more secure than that. All the cameras and the alarm are hooked up to a battery backup in the basement."

After restoring the power, I get a piece of scrap wood from the garage and board up the window on the kitchen door. Then I get the basement ready for Lindsey's return and pack my clothes for the trip. The last thing I need to do is take out the cash from my safe. Even though I know no one else is home, I follow the same routine I do each time that I go into the spare bedroom.

Looking around, I confirm no one else is there, then I enter the code on the keypad of the lock and push open the door. My computer setup, comfy chair and a locked filing cabinet are the only things visible in the room. I log on to the computer and, after rewatching it, I erase the footage of Claire and Lindsey taking off. I send a quick email to my older brother, Brock, to let him know that I was headed home for a visit. I know that he will let our mom know because she has no email and after all, he is back living in her trailer with her. He got out of jail six months ago and his emails since getting out have been constantly complaining. I have been sure to only reply with positive comments on how great my life in Denver is.

My brother, Brock and I were close when we were kids, but since the first time he went to jail when he was twenty, we have drifted apart. He never stays out of lock up for long, so it seems useless to try to really connect with the guy. Stealing cars and getting into bar fights has been a way of life for him for almost ten years and it seems he will never learn the lesson the law is trying to teach him by locking him up.

I shut down the computer and walk to the filing cabinet. The lock is a fingerprint scanner so even if someone got into this room, they wouldn't be able to open the cabinet. I slide open the top drawer and look at the two hanging files inside. One is of no use to me today, but the other one in front contains the key to the safe that I installed in the closet. I'm sure most people would find my set up to be over the top, but I never want Lindsey to get her hands on the things I have in this room, least of all the money in the safe.

I stare into the safe and wonder whether I should take all the money with me. Rocky officially pays me minimum wage, so my paychecks actually suck, but the real deal is that he pays me mostly in cash. He offers discounts to customers who pay cash, so most people pay that way and I'm sure that these sales don't get reported on his taxes since we have a separate cash register for them. I do not know how my cousin handles taxes and crap since marijuana is still considered an illegal drug by the feds, and I honestly don't care. The other file in my cabinet is on Rocky and the cash sales at his business. I have taken pictures and documented all the cash sales totals since I started there. I consider this file to be an insurance policy; in case Rocky ever tries to screw me over.

I have just over one hundred thousand dollars in cash, but that seems like too much to bring. I go back and forth in my mind. I do not know how long it will take me to find Lindsey and get her back here. I unzip the duffel bag sitting next to the safe and carefully put all the money into it. Running out of cash could put a real kink in my plans, so taking it all seems to be the right call.

After locking everything back up, I get in my truck and hit the road. I am no longer worried about the head start the girls have on me. I don't plan to go right to Claire's house, anyway. No, I want Lindsey to settle in and start to believe she is safe before I grab her. I will watch her then when she is least expecting it, I will bounce. I need to call Rocky and tell him I am not sure when I will be back, but that can wait, too. I drive into the night and daydream about the reunion that Lindsey and I will have.

As I drive into the darkness, I think about the first time I met Claire. I had heard her name a bunch of times from Lindsey, but I wasn't really prepared when I met her. Claire could be described as gorgeous and I thought that until I spent time with her. Despite her good looks, petite frame and long shiny red hair, her attitude ruined all of that. Claire was anything but the complete package. No, she was like one of those restaurants that looks fabulous on the outside, but then you eat the meal and it is beyond disappointing. With Claire, I knew that first time we met that we weren't going to get along, but whatever, I wasn't dating her.

The thing with Claire is she has an opinion about everything and feels the need to share it. It doesn't help that Lindsey told me that Claire isn't even sure she ever wants to be married or have kids. I mean, come on, what kind of woman thinks like that? I asked Lindsey a bunch of times if Claire had ever hit on her because I've come to the conclusion that she must be a lesbian. Lindsey always denied that, but it adds up to me. Her whole independent woman, I don't need a man attitude. She has always been a bad influence on Lindsey.

12

Homecoming

Sunday, March 3, 2024
Claire

Home sweet home, I think as I pull into the garage and turn off the SUV. Lindsey has barely spoken, eaten, or been awake since we left Hays, Kansas. Whatever Mack did to her over the last two years has left her practically catatonic. She stirs next to me and startles awake as she has every time she has woken up on this trip. I take her hand in mine and rub the back of it the way my mom used to rub mine when I was little and scared. Lindsey turns and almost smiles at me.

"Do my folks know I am here?" she says in that thin, defeated voice that seems to be all she has left.

"Not yet. I wanted you to decide when and how to tell them."

"Thanks for that, but I think we need to get my dad to help us. Mack is dangerous and he will come looking for me."

"Okay, let's go inside and call them together." We walk in hand in hand through the kitchen door as we have hundreds of times before. I'm so glad my best friend is here with me, but I am worried about her and I haven't even asked her what happened. She is so skittish, and I don't want to upset her. I wonder if she is right that Mack will come after her. I mean, after all, what kind of guy would chase a woman across several states? That is just nuts.

After we get into the house, Lindsey goes to take a shower and change her clothes and I call her mom. I have known Jana Peterson almost as long as I have Lindsey and she is like a second mom to me.

"Mrs. Peterson, it's Claire."

"Yes, honey, I know who it is, and I told you to call me Jana. What's going on?"

"I just got back from Denver and I have Lindsey with me."

"WHAT?! Lindsey is there."

"Yes, she is in the shower but Mrs. Peterson she is in really rough shape and doesn't seem ready to talk about whatever went on."

"Okay, I am going to call her dad and then we will be over there."

"Alright, see you soon."

"Claire, thank you for getting my little girl back."

After hanging up the phone, I started coffee and fed the cats, Monica and Rachel. Lindsey and I got the cats when she lived with me before Mack took her to Colorado. While she has been gone, the cats have been a reminder of her every day. The shower stops running, so I go to tell Lindsey that her mom and dad are on the way over. She says ok through the bathroom door then nothing else, so I head to the basement to start my laundry. The one thing that I would change about this house is the laundry in the basement. My mom and dad moved into the house when I was little, and my dad added a laundry chute, which helps but still the basement is creepy.

I stand next to the washing machine, staring at the cinderblock wall. The hopeless feeling I have just won't pass. I may have saved Lindsey physically, but I'm pretty sure someone else will need to save her emotionally and mentally. I have never understood why women stay with or go back to an abusive partner. Lindsey, being my best friend, only adds to that bewilderment for me.

As the washing machine begins to spin, I think back to when I met Lindsey in kindergarten. My mom and I watched as a moving truck arrived down the block and people's stuff was carried into the house. I remember telling my mom that my new best friend just moved in and she laughed because we had not even met the family that was moving in yet. But I had seen the pink canopy bed and giant rainbow unicorn being carried in and knew that whoever the girl moving in was, she was cool. Two days later, my parents took me to the school open house, and that is when I officially met Lindsey and her parents.

I didn't need to be introduced to her to know it was our new neighbors. Lindsey had a Lisa Frank backpack, folders, and hair ribbons. She was the epitome of five-year-old coolness. I knew back then and still know that Lindsey was the best friend I would ever have. I feel the tears sliding down my face as I think about the broken version of that cool little girl who is upstairs waiting for her mom and dad to come over.

13

The Hug

Sunday March 3, 2024
Lindsey

I listen to Claire's retreating footsteps before I open the bathroom door. I thought about using some of her makeup to hide the worst of my bruises, but she is so much paler than me it was a bad idea. Plus, if my folks were going to help me, they need to understand that Mack was holding me hostage and hurting me. I know they are both pissed that I took off with him, but now that I am back, I hope they get over that quickly. Because whether or not Claire believes me, Mack is on his way and I obviously can't stop him on my own.

Half an hour ago, when I first walked into the bedroom that was mine before I left with Mack, it was a relief and a surprise to find that Claire hadn't changed anything. The clothes and other things I left behind are still right where I left them. The only difference is that the note I left her is now sitting on the top of my dresser instead of on the kitchen table. I look at the note and think how stupid I was to ever trust Mack. I chose him over my best friend and parents. I stare at the note that reads:

Claire,
I am leaving with Mack. Please, just leave us alone and try to be
happy for us. We love each other and have forgiven each other for
the mistakes we have both made in the past. -   Lindsey.

The note seems ridiculous in light of the past two years and I can't
for the life of me remember what Mack had forgiven me for. I now
know that was one of the manipulative ways Mack turned his abuse
into my fault. I try to think back to when I realized that his abuse was
about something that is wrong with him and not something that is
wrong with me. As I stand there bracing myself on the dresser, it hits
me that wasn't one moment. It happened slowly. Every mean word,
every kick, every punch took a little more of my soul. When we first
got to Colorado, I wondered after each time what I could have done
differently and then I would try to change, so I didn't make Mack
mad. It had slowly dawned on me that I could never stop Mack.

I'm just pulling on one of my old hoodies and a pair of sweatpants
when I hear the doorbell ring, then Claire running up the basement
steps and the front door opening. For a brief moment, I consider locking the bedroom door and going to bed, but that would be just putting
off the inevitable. I take a deep breath and walk into the family room.
My parents are sitting on the couch holding hands until they see me
and they both spring up at the same time. My dad is in his uniform
so he is likely on duty and my mom is wearing what over the years
has become her uniform of choice, black yoga pants and an oversized
sweatshirt. Over the last few years, when I have become anxious about
what is about to happen, life seems to be in slow motion. I see every
movement that my mom makes and hear her ask, "Lindsey? Is it okay
if I hug you?"

I nod my head as I don't trust myself to not start crying if I try
talking. I feel her arms envelop me and her scent rush into my senses.
Being hugged by your mother is something that can instantly take you

back to childhood. My mom has worn Happy perfume, washed her hair with a citrus scented shampoo and put Oil of Olay on her face twice a day for as long as I can remember. These products help to make the scent that is so uniquely her. I feel my body relaxing for the first time in years and begin to sob in her arms. My dad wraps himself around both of us and my sobbing only deepens. *How could I have been so stupid to leave with Mack?*

As my parents pull away, I feel the loss of their warmth and strength before I register that my mom is talking to me.

"I'm sorry, mom, can you repeat that?"

"Lindsey, we both love you so much and have been ever so worried about you. Claire said that you aren't ready to talk about what has been going on so we won't push, but honey, you don't look well. Will you please come with us to the hospital and get checked out?"

"Mom, I don't need a hospital."

"Please, just do it for our peace of mind."

The tone of her voice is the one she uses when she isn't going to take no for an answer. I know I am better off to go with them now because if I refuse, she will just badger me until I agree. "Alright, I will go, but I am telling you that there is nothing wrong with me."

Claire is standing in the hallway with a tray full of coffee mugs. "Do you want me to come with you?" she asks as she sets the tray down on the hall table.

"No, it will be fine. I know you have to work tomorrow and we both know how slow hospitals can be. Is the alarm code still the same? And can I have my key back?"

"Yeah, the code is still the same, but I think we should change it just in case you ever mentioned it to Mack. Your key is right here in this drawer. It has been waiting for you to come back."

I hug her and realize how blessed I am to have Claire as my best friend even if I could not stand her at first way back in kindergarten.

14

The Trailer Park

Sunday March 3, 2024

Mack

The thing about growing up in a trailer park is that you don't expect progress when you return. The park doesn't disappoint in its sameness, dullness, lack of hope that it exudes. I park my truck right in front of my mom's place. My mom's twenty-year-old Honda is in its usual spot. I remember when she bought the car because it was also the year my dad went to prison for the rest of his life. She was super proud of the car. It was only six months old with less than ten thousand miles and I think that with my dad finally out of the picture, she felt like she deserved something nice. The paint is faded now and there are some dings, but last I heard it still runs tip top.

I knock once on the door and turn the handle to open it. I don't know that my mom has ever locked that door. Mom is sitting in her recliner watching her afternoon talk show. It's four in the afternoon and mom works at the diner from five in the morning until two in the afternoon, so I knew that she would be home. To look at my mom, you would think she was frail, but she is the toughest old broad I have ever met. She seems to survive on cigarettes and black coffee, but I also know she loves the french fries at the diner and has a basket every shift she works. She survived an alcoholic, criminal, abusive husband who rarely brought any money into the house, all while raising three sons.

"Hi, mom."

"Well, there you are. Brock said you were coming for a visit. Did you bring that stuck up girlfriend of yours?"

"Lindsey is not stuck up, and she is visiting her folks while I visit you," I say with a sigh.

"Hmmm, are you planning to stay here?"

"Yes, mom."

"Just you or the two of you?"

"Just me, mom. Is Brock here?"

"No, he is meeting with his parole officer. At least one of you made me proud and has stayed out of prison."

"Thanks, mom, I guess in this family success is measured by lacking a felony."

We both start laughing at the same time.

"So, how is Chet doing in prison?" I ask my mom when we both stop laughing.

"You would know if you ever bothered to go see him or at least write a letter. But since you don't, I guess I'll tell you. He got moved to the same cell block as your dad six months or so back. According to Chet, that made his life a lot better because no one messes with LeRoy. Hopefully Chet will stay infraction free so he can be eligible for parole, eventually."

"Do you see both of them when you go up there, or just Chet?"

"With the price of gas being what it is, I don't go see none of those deadbeats. Chet writes to me almost every week and I write him back. When I have a little extra money, I put it on his books so he can get something at the commissary."

"Ma, I'm glad you stay in touch with him, and he is my older brother, but he and I weren't close when he got sent away and I don't see us ever becoming that way. If it is okay with you, I am going to go lay down for a bit. When I get up, I will take you to get some dinner. How does that sound?"

"As long as it isn't to the diner, it sounds good to me. I put fresh sheets on your bed so your room is all ready for you."

I wake up a couple of hours later when I hear the front door slam shut. When I make it out to the living and dining area, I see Brock and my mom sitting at the table eating fried chicken from a fast-food joint. I grab a drumstick out of the bucket before I sit down.

"I guess I won't be taking you out for dinner after all."

Brock shrugs and says, "My parole officer was all up on me because I still don't have a job, so I stopped at this place and applied just so he will shut up about it next week. Anyway, I am sitting there filling out the application and the chicken smell was making me super hungry, so I grabbed us some. I wasn't aware you had big plans."

I chuckle and reply, "No big deal. The chicken sounds good to me as long as ma is happy."

Mom smiles and says, "Any dinner that I didn't have to cook or carry out to a table is a great meal for me."

When we finish up the food, I clean up and then sit back on the couch. "Hey ma, is it okay with you if I take your car when I go out for a bit?"

"Why not take your truck?" Brock comments even though no one was talking to him.

"Not that it is your business, a knock started from the engine just as I was getting to town. I am going to take a look at it tomorrow morning, but I want to go over to the bar and catch up with some of the guys tonight."

"Just be sure my car is back with a full tank of gas by four am because I am opening the diner tomorrow," mom says before she unmutes the TV and starts watching a reality show. The show is about marrying someone you don't know. Like that isn't a recipe for disaster.

I have no plans to go to a bar, so I'm surprised and relieved when Brock doesn't try to invite himself along. I'm headed over to Claire's place to start to figure out if that is where Lindsey is. I need to know where she is to make a plan. It is going to be more complicated if she ran back to her cop daddy, but I will get her back no matter what.

15

There Is Work To Be Done

Monday March 4, 2024
Claire

I know Lindsey got back a little after midnight because the security camera system alerted me when she walked up to the front door. I sat up and watched her parents hug her before her dad opened the door. He went in and Lindsey and her mom stood on the porch with Lindsey leaning against her mom. I guessed he was checking the house to be sure Mack wasn't there. He opened my door slowly and saw me sitting up, staring at my phone.

He leaned against the door frame and says, "Claire, Mrs. Peterson and I can't thank you enough for going after Lindsey, but I would be remiss if I didn't tell you that what you did was very dangerous. You should have told us what was going on and I would have gone with you and gotten police assistance. It is late so I am going to go get Lindsey and her mom, but tomorrow, please go see Jana so she can fill you in on what the doctor and social worker had to say. Will you please do that for Lindsey?"

I wonder if Dan Peterson will call my dad at some point and tell him what I did. I nod my head when he is done talking. "I have to be at work at seven, but will plan to go by your house when I am done. Is that okay?"

"I'll have Jana stop in and let you know before we leave." he says as he steps out of my room and gently closes the door.

I continue to watch the front door camera until I see Mr. Peterson walk outside and escort both Lindsey and her mom in. The last thing I see before I close the app is an older, maroon car driving by slowly.

This morning, the only thing I changed from my normal work day routine is writing a note to Lindsey before I left. I am sitting at my desk in my cubicle in the CSI department area sorting through five days' worth of emails when my cell phone pings. It is a team text message for us to report to a crime scene. It is the best part of the job, actually gathering evidence and analyzing it. The endless paperwork is the worst part, or maybe it is the meetings.

I grab my gear bag and head to the van that the CSI team uses. The rest of my team all arrive at about the same moment that I do. We climb into the van; I take my usual place in the front passenger seat and put the address of the crime scene into the navigation system. The conversation in the van is around what people did the last few days.

Cal is driving, but he has no trouble multitasking and animatedly telling all of us about his fishing escapade with his brother. When he is done, he asks, "So, what about you Claire, what did you get up to the last few days?"

I hadn't planned to join in on the conversation because how could I possibly put into words the last few days, but I also don't want to be rude. "I went to Denver to visit a long-time friend."

From the back seat, April another tech replies, "Wow, that is a long drive. Did you go alone?"

"I drove there by myself, but my friend Lindsey decided to ride back with me so she could visit her folks."

Matt, who is sitting next to April, says, "That's cool. I just binged on a Netflix series and slept."

I am relieved that we are pulling up to the address, so the conversation is dropped. I pull up the information that we have so far on the department issued tablet and read to my team.

"This is a possible homicide of an eighty-three-year-old female, presumably the homeowner Hazel Green. The lead detective is Kass Minor. That is all we have for now. Does anyone have questions?"

The rest of the team indicates that there are no questions. We have worked as a team long enough to know what roles each of us will play. Matt takes crime scene photos, April marks potential evidence with numbered flags, Cal collects the marked evidence and I control the scene. That means that I make sure everyone there is logged in and everyone's movements at the scene are recorded. I am standing by the front door when Detective Minor approaches me.

"Hi, Claire. How are you doing today?"

"Fine, thanks and you, Detective Minor?" She doesn't look well. I wonder if it is a particularly gory crime scene.

"I have a sick kid at home and just want to take a nap, but other than that, I am good. I'm not sure this is a crime scene, but since this was an unexpected death, we will all play it safe. Like every unexplained death, we will investigate this as a homicide until we can rule out that it wasn't one."

"What makes you wonder if it isn't a crime?"

"The victim, Hazel Green, is tucked into her bed like she went to sleep and just never woke up. Her son, who lives in Kansas City, called in a wellness check when she didn't answer his calls. The front and back doors were locked when the patrol officer responded. The son also called his sister, who wasn't that worried at first, but when he told her he had called the police, she also responded to the scene and gave the officer the key she had and permission to enter. When the officer found Hazel dead in her bed, he called for backup. The fire department cleared the house because there was no sign of a carbon monoxide leak. There is also no sign of a struggle or a robbery,"

I know that a lot of detectives don't share this much with crime scene techs, but Kass Minor and I have a deeper relationship. She is the detective that solved my mom's murder and I will forever be grateful to her. "That sounds like she could have died of natural causes. I noticed that the ME, Doctor Reeves, isn't here yet. When are you expecting him?"

Minor tilts her head to the right and I look that way to see the ME van pull up. She smiles and walks towards the van.

I spend the rest of the workday with my team at the scene gathering evidence and then logging it all in back at the department. At three o'clock, my team and I clock out for the day. Jana Peterson stopped in my room last night and said to stop by after work, so that is where I'm headed before going home. I hope Lindsey won't be upset that I am talking with her mom without her there.

16

Dependency

Monday March 4, 2024
Lindsey

Last night, I actually set the alarm on the cell phone that Claire bought me back in Kansas. I can't remember the last time I set an alarm, but I know my mom will be here at 11:15 to take me to the two appointments that I agreed to last night. The doctor at the emergency room wanted to admit me for malnutrition but I was adamant that I did not want that. So, the compromise was that I would meet with a dietitian and a counselor today.

In the kitchen, I find a note from Claire. She changed the alarm code to her birth month and my birthday. I start a fresh pot of coffee and eat an apple and a cheese stick. The doctor last night warned me that I can't simply go back to eating like I did before Mack. She said that my body would likely reject too much food at once. That is the main reason I am seeing the dietitian. I know that I am too thin but I also know that I don't want to get fat. So, I will take whatever she has to say with a grain of salt.

I am not sure how a counselor is going to help me, but the doctor insisted saying that she was diagnosing me with probable PTSD. I wanted to say, 'Well duh. I have been held prisoner for the last year by a man who claimed to love me and showed that by starving and beating me'. But I didn't say that since both of my parents were standing in the room and were both nodding. I certainly don't need a counselor to tell me that I made bad choices since getting involved with Mack or that he is responsible for the choices he made. Despite that, I will go to that appointment too because what else do I have to do.

After dressing in a pair of sweatpants and a t-shirt that I left behind when I moved to Colorado, the clothes are beyond baggy and I can barely keep the pants up even with the string tied as tight as it will go but I have nothing else to wear. I head to the kitchen for a cup of coffee. Once I sit down in the living room, I turn on the television to a morning news show and let it play in the background while my mind wanders. I have no money, no job and I look horrible, so I am not sure how to start getting back on my feet. Nevertheless, I know I am lucky because I am away from Mack. The problem is, I have an intense burning in my stomach and a mantra running through my head that is like a warning alarm going off. That alarm is shouting over and over, 'He is going to kill you!' but that is not what worries me the most. I brought this on myself, so if, no, when Mack kills me, I will deserve it but Claire. Claire has only been a good friend to me, and I don't know how to keep her safe.

I am thinking about the pros and cons of asking my parents if I can stay there when the doorbell rings. I scream and almost run towards the bedrooms when I realize that it is probably my mom. I have to force myself to walk up to the door and look through the window. A whoosh of relief floods my body as I see mom out on the front porch. I turn off the alarm, unlock the door, and motion for her to come in. Before we leave, I go to the kitchen and flip Claire's note over. I scribble down, *Ask Claire for APP to watch the camera on my phone.* Then I head back to where my mom is standing in the hall. It is only then that I see she is holding two large shopping bags.

"What's in the bags, mom?"

"You know I love to shop and Claire mentioned last night that you didn't have a lot of clothes, so this morning I hit a few shops before coming over here. I hope that's okay?"

I can hear the hesitation in her voice and although her taste in clothes is not usually mine, I know it is one of the ways she shows love. "Of course it is, mom. It was very nice of you because I don't have much and I am not ready to go shopping." I don't add, but I'm sure she suspects that I also have no money, so even if I felt like going, I couldn't. I set the alarm, lock the front door, and we walk out together. She parked her car right in front of the house, which is funny to me since her house is only two houses away.

"You don't have to drive over here. We can walk back to your house and get the car."

"I told you I went shopping before I came here, but I'll keep that in mind for next time."

We ride in silence the rest of the time until we turn on the road for the hospital where both my appointments are and my mom asks, "Do you want me to come with you or do you want to let me know when you are done and I will pick you up?"

I would love to tell her that I can do this without her, but I just can't. I fear that Mack is watching me and if I am alone, he will snatch me. I rationally know that I will be in a public place that likely has security, but I am afraid. I hear myself saying in a low, trembling voice, 'Please come with me.' and I feel my mom touching my arm, but I am too trapped in my fear to process any of it.

When my mom opens the car door on my side, I startle and almost scream again. It is the smell of her that keeps me grounded enough to know it is not Mack. I unbuckle my seatbelt and take her outstretched hand as I step out of the car. I continue to hold her hand all the way to the dietitian's office.

I leave that appointment with a stack of papers and a plan. I agreed to add two hundred and fifty to three hundred calories a day for the next two weeks and not to weigh myself. The last part isn't that hard for me because I'm pretty sure that Claire doesn't even own a scale. As we sit and wait for the counselor, mom asks if I want anything to eat or drink.

I am about to tell her a black coffee when I think about what the dietitian said. "When I go back to see the counselor, would you be willing to go to Starbucks and get me a Caramel Macchiato?"

"Of course I will. Do you want it to be a skinny or regular?" she asks in a tone that can only be described as a cross between surprised and excited.

As much as I want to say skinny, I know that a regular drink will add all the calories I agreed to and I won't have to worry about eating more or breaking my promise. "I will take a tall regular one. Thanks, mom"

"You don't have to thank me. It is not a big deal. There is a Starbucks next door and I am happy to do anything that helps you."

I am about to tell her that I meant thank you not just for the drink but for everything. I also want to tell her how sorry I am for my bad choices, but before I can, I hear my name being called. I see a woman about my mom's age wearing a sweater set and jeans. My mom squeezes my hand as I stand up and I give her what I hope is a reassuring smile.

17

Trucks, Van, and Plans

Monday March 4, 2024

Mack

When I wake up in my childhood bedroom in my twin size bed, I still haven't come up with a plan for how to get Lindsey. However, I know for sure that she is staying with Claire and that her parents know she is back. I drove by Claire's house a half dozen times last night and on the last time, I finally spotted Lindsey. She was with her mom and dad, walking through the front door. The one thing that I know for sure is that I will need to get a new vehicle. I can't keep driving my mom's car and Lindsey and Claire both know my truck, so that isn't a choice. Plus, a cargo van will be a much better choice for getting Lindsey back home.

After a shower, getting dressed and grabbing some cash, I find Brock sitting in the living room playing a video game. There are several empty Mountain Dew cans and an ashtray full of cigarette butts sitting on the coffee table next to him. He looks up as I walk in and pauses his game. "Do you need some help with the truck?"

"Nah, that old thing has over two hundred thousand miles on it, so I am going to sell it and get something else." I say without thinking about how to explain having money to buy a new vehicle.

"Must be nice to be a JJ Moneybags." He jokingly replies as he returns to the video game.

I grab a soda out of the fridge and head out the door. My first stop is the diner that mom works at for a bite to eat. I use the free Wi-Fi at the diner to search for vans and narrow it down to a few choices. I pay my bill and hand my mom a tip that is double the bill. She smiles at me and tries to hand the money back. I shake my head and she shoves the money into her apron's front pocket. Brock texts me just as I am leaving;

Hey bro-Let me know what they will give you for your truck. I might want to buy it.

I have to think about my reply because I have no idea where Brock would get any money from and figure that he really just wants me to give him my truck. The thing is, I could just give him the truck if I wanted to, but the problem is I'm not sure I want to. The guy needs to get a job and quit depending on everyone else to take care of him. He is in his mid-thirties and lives like a fifteen-year-old kid. I keep my reply short and noncommittal.

I'll let you know

The second van I look at is the one I buy. It is perfect for me. Dark blue, no rear windows and it used to belong to a mobile dog grooming business. The previous owners had modified the van with hooks for leashes, an area that a cage locks into, a sink area with a large floor drain and a tank for water. The salesman at the lot took a grand off the price since I didn't require them to remove the modifications. I texted Brock as they wrote up the paperwork.

I'll be back at the trailer in twenty if you really want the truck. Then you can drive me back to get the van that I just bought.

Almost immediately, the three dots indicating he was writing back appeared.

How much for the truck?

I was going to tell him I hadn't even asked what they would give me on trade and that he could just have the truck. But since he asked, I respond,

A grand

Brock sends back a thumbs up emoji and I head over to the trailer to pick him up. I wondered if he would ask why I wanted a van and I planned to tell him the same thing that I had told the sales guy at the dealership. When I get back to Denver, I am going to start delivering for Amazon. So many people make money off the gig economy that it seems like a plausible reason.

Brock jumps into the passenger seat of my truck and hands me a wad of money. I had been thinking that he was going to try to talk me into payments, but it seems he has the cash. I'm sure it is not from any legit sources since he doesn't have a job, but I really don't want to know, so I don't ask. I'm lost in thought when Brock starts talking.

"I don't hear a knock in the engine. Did you fix it and still decide to get something else?"

Leave it to Brock to actually remember something I said only when I wish he wouldn't. "Nah, I think it was some bad gas. I stopped for gas at a sketchy place just over the border and it started running rough after that. Now that it has good ol' Missouri gas in it, she's running fine. But I had already started thinking about getting a van, so I figured I might as well go ahead."

Brock nods but doesn't reply. Something about the way he is looking at me tells me that he doesn't completely believe what I'm saying. That's okay, I never completely believe what he says either. With Brock, it is always part bullshit with maybe a sprinkle of truth.

"So, this morning after you left, your girlfriend's cop dad stopped by looking for you."

"Oh yeah, what did you tell him?"

"That I don't talk to pigs."

"I bet that went over well."

"He said to tell you to stay away from Lindsey. So, brother, want to tell me what's going on? Because I know you told mom that you and Lindsey were just visiting. Also, mom told me like three years ago that while I was locked up, Lindsey got a restraining order against you."

"That was just a misunderstanding. Just like this is. We had a petty argument, and she ran home to mommy and daddy."

"So, what are you going to do about it?"

"I'm working on it."

"Oh, I bet you are."

18

Moms and Muffins

Monday March 4, 2024
Claire

I knock on the front door of the Peterson's house like I have so many times before, but this is different because I know Lindsey is at my house. Jana Peterson answers the door wearing her baking apron and the scent of her double chocolate muffins wafts out onto the porch.

"Thank you for stopping by Claire. I want you to know that I told Lindsey that her dad and I asked you to come here this afternoon, so you aren't hiding anything from her."

Although I wonder how she knew that I was worried about this, I don't ask. I follow her into the living room, where she has set out the muffins and some coffee. I remember my mom used to joke that Jana Peterson was a modern-day June Cleaver and that I never really understood the reference until one day I googled it. Jana stayed at home until Lindsey started school and then she went back to decorating cakes for bakeries. She does some really cool, elaborate designs. She was always the room mother when we were in elementary school and there were always freshly baked goodies when I was over.

"Dan and I can't begin to express how grateful we are for you bringing Lindsey back to us. I know he already chastised you for going alone, so I won't do it, too. We think it is important that you know what the staff at the emergency room told us last night and how they suggested we best support Lindsey."

"Okay, I will do whatever is going to help her the most." I say nodding my head, then pick up a muffin, pinch off a piece of the top and pop it in my mouth.

"Lindsey is very malnourished, which you could probably tell just by looking at her. The doctor last night wanted to admit her for nutritional therapy, but Lindsey refused. She saw a dietitian today who gave her very specific instructions for how to increase her calorie count overtime to ease her body back into a normal eating pattern. Don't be surprised if she continues to eat very little for a while. Mack literally starved her so her body can't take much food right now."

Jana has tears streaking down her face, and I hand her a napkin from the coffee table. Other than that, I am at a loss for what to do or say, so I just sit there and wait for her to continue talking.

"Sorry, I just feel like I failed her. I thought we had raised her to be a strong, independent woman, but she was not that. She is a broken shell of the woman who left with that piece of crap. Lindsey gave the doctor and social worker permission to talk to her dad and I but not to share specifics. They both told us that she has suffered severe abuse, that included physical torture and mental and emotional abuse. The social worker told us that Lindsey is blaming herself because Mack gaslighted her for two years to believe that she brought all of it on herself."

So far, nothing Mrs. Peterson has said is a surprise to me. Maybe she didn't see the changes in Lindsey before she left, but I did, or maybe she doesn't want to admit to having ignored the signs. I mean, come on, no reasonable person would willingly start drinking black coffee instead of lattes, but Lindsey did. Also, when she started jogging, there was no way anyone who knew her should have thought that was her idea. Throughout middle and high school, I tried to get her to join sports with me, but she never would. She always told me that she hated feeling sweaty. I don't point any of this out to Mrs. Peterson, instead, I just nod.

"I think the hardest thing for me to hear was that Lindsey likely will go back to him."

Startled by this, I shout, "WHAT? After what we just went through and all that Lindsey has endured, how could anyone think she would go back to that POS?"

Jana is crying harder, so she takes a few minutes to continue. I sit there staring and wonder if all that I did will be for nothing.

"Sorry about that. The social worker said that on average, women leave their abuser seven times before they stay separated from them. She also said that Lindsey was clear that she believes that he will come here and kill her. The social worker said that twenty percent of women who leave their abusive partner are murdered by that partner. Dan persuaded Lindsey to file for an emergency order of protection. The thing is that neither the social worker nor Dan had to tell me that the order is not likely to deter that monster."

Now both Mrs. Peterson and I are crying, and I don't know how to respond to what she had just told me. Finally, I take a few deep breaths and ask, "What can I do to help her?"

Mrs. Peterson and I talked for about an hour, and when I leave, I have a clearer picture of the reality of domestic violence. You would think working for the Springfield Police Department, I would know this stuff, but CSI techs really don't get called in on those kinds of cases. During our talk, Mrs. Peterson told me several times how dangerous these situations are but especially how worried they were about Mack in particular. His family has a history of violence with both his dad and oldest brother in prison for murder.

19

New Evidence

Tuesday March 5, 2024
Claire

I sit at my desk after finishing up the preliminary report on the evidence from the Hazel Green case, waiting for my shift to end. I look up and see Detective Minor walking towards me. She doesn't seem to be feeling any better today.

"Hi, are you available to return to Green house with me?"

"Like right now?" I'm not sure why I ask like that because it is pretty obvious that she walked up here so we could go right now.

Nodding her head, Detective Minor adds, "Mrs. Green's son, Howard, called me about ten minutes ago. He and his sister Harriet are going through their mom's house to be sure nothing was stolen, like I asked them to. Howard tells me that his mom kept large amounts of cash in a shoe box in her closet. The shoe box is still there but there is no money in it. I read your preliminary report and neither the shoe box nor the closet was dusted for prints."

Feeling my defenses rise, I temper my voice, "Which closet? Was there a sign of disturbance in that area? Because I remember the house looking like there was nothing out of place. Aside from Mrs. Green's dead body, of course."

"I remember the house the same way and your team's photographs back that up. Howard said she kept the shoe box in her bedroom closet. When I pressed him, he admitted that neither he nor his sister had actually seen their mom take or put money in it since they moved out decades ago. However, I would like to cover all our bases in case the medical examiner comes back with a cause of death other than natural causes. So, are you available, or can you get one of your other team members to accompany me over there?"

I think about Abe, the forensic IT guy I have been seeing for a while, and our plan to have dinner tonight. The greatest thing about dating another member of the police department is that they totally get when something comes up. I stand up and reply, "I will go grab a kit and join you there."

Detective Minor smiles replying, "Thanks, see you there in a few minutes."

After grabbing my finger print kit, camera and tablet, I shoot a quick text to Lindsey and one to Abe. Then I email my boss regarding where I'm headed and why I need to go back over to the Green crime scene. The email is really just a professional courtesy since Hugh, my boss, doesn't keep that close an eye on any of us in the department.

Pulling up to Hazel Green's former residence, I spot Detective Minor waiting by her car. We walk in together and the detective introduces me to Hazel's kids.

"It is like I told you on the phone, Detective Minor. My mom always kept a lot of cash in the house. You see, mom never learned to drive and wanted to have access to her money without having to rely on anyone to take her to the bank. Let me show you where the shoe box that she kept the money is." Howard then led us to the main bedroom.

Unlike the last time we were here, the closet door is open. Sitting on the top of a small dresser is a shoe box.

Harriet had come with us to the bedroom and spoke for the first time since we arrived. "I'm afraid both my brother and I touched it, but we put it back where we found it. When you open it, you will see there are my mom's important papers in it, but no money. I'm sure Howard told you that we can't be certain how much money or really if there was any money in it. But we both agree it would be strange for mom to have changed her habits."

I get to work by first taking pictures of the closet and the shoe box, then dusting for fingerprints. I already got prints to rule out Harriet when we were here the other day and Howard was in the system because he worked for a defense contractor, so I don't need those either. We have several prints that are currently of unknown origin. The house is what I believe is called shotgun style. There are many of them in this area of town and it makes it so I can clearly hear the conversation going on in the living room.

"Who, other than the two of you, knows about the money your mom kept here?" Detective Minor asks.

I don't hear a reply, but based on what Howard says next, I assume they both shook their heads to indicate that they don't know. "Mom had hired a local guy to help out with the lawn and do some basic maintenance so he would have had access to the house. She got Meals on Wheels delivered a couple times a week and a visiting nurse came by weekly to help with her medication and oxygen. Otherwise, I can't think of anyone else who would have been in here to even have an opportunity to see the cash. How about you Harriet?"

"Well, I try to come over at least once a week and take her grocery shopping, but yeah, I think you covered everyone else. But I can't imagine mom letting them see the money."

I am packing up my supplies when I hear Detective Minor ask if either Howard or Harriet have names and contact information for the people they mentioned. As I enter the living room, I see Harriet take a piece of paper off the refrigerator and hand it to Detective Minor.

"CSI Learner, will you please take a photo of this for evidentiary purposes?"

I nod and take a quick picture. The paper contains ten names and phone numbers in neat rows. I wonder if the people whose fingerprints I haven't identified yet are on this list or, for that matter, the killer. The first seven entries are doctor's offices, a bank, the utility company, a pharmacy, and the cable company, so no one who will probably have fingerprints in the house. The next entries were for a Katie McQueen-Visiting Nurse, and Meals on Wheels. The last entry was a single name: Brock, with a phone number. I'm sure that Detective Minor will have me gather more fingerprints in the very near future.

20

Porch Sitting

Tuesday March 5, 2024
Lindsey

The counselor I talked to yesterday is nice enough, and we didn't get into the heavy stuff. I'm supposed to be thinking about my goals and being kind to myself before my next appointment. What exactly it means to be kind to myself is a mystery to me, but I figure putting flavored creamer in my coffee is a good start. Here I am, back in the bedroom with my coffee, staring at the bags my mom brought by yesterday.

I dump all the clothes onto the bed and begin sorting through them. There are four pairs of black leggings, four graphic t-shirts of bands I loved as a teen, two hoodies, packages of sports bras, underwear and socks. Mom did great with her choices, so I cut off the tags and changed into a new outfit. I look in the mirror and for a brief moment consider cutting my hair short. Mack loved it long and I don't want to continue to look a certain way just because he said so. Then, I remember our freshmen year of high school, when Claire and I decided to cut each other's hair into the Rachel haircut.

We used photos from the internet and both cuts turned out horribly. Our mothers were kind enough to not be mean about the haircuts. We both ended up with short bob haircuts and it is the last real haircut I got. I used to get my hair trimmed a few times a year, but in the last year and a half it hasn't even been trimmed. I stop short of going to get a pair of scissors and decide instead to get a professional cut once I get a job. Last night at the emergency room, my dad gave me a credit card to use and told me that he would have one sent with my name on it. I know he wouldn't ever say anything if I charged a haircut, but I only ever intend to use the card in an emergency.

Instead, I head out to the porch like I did yesterday, but this time I take the old laptop that I left here with me. Claire left me instructions on how to load the app for the camera system onto both my phone and the laptop. I cue up the cameras and study the live feed and the different angles that each camera shows. I walk around the house three times and then go back to the porch to watch the recordings. Now I know all the spots that are recorded and the ones that aren't.

I push the porch seat to be right in the camera's view. As I'm settling back into the chair, I see my mom walking towards the house. She is carrying a Starbucks coffee cup and a small container.

"Good morning, sweetheart."

"Morning, mom."

She sets the coffee cup and container on the table next to me before she sits in the other chair. I pick up the container and open the lid. The scent of cinnamon and apples wafts up towards me. I peer in and see four mini muffins.

"I made your favorite apple strudel muffins." she says with a hint of expectation in her voice.

"Thanks, they smell divine." I pinch a piece off the top of one of them and pop it in my mouth.

"You're welcome. Do you have any plans for today?"

"No, not really."

"I'm headed to the food pantry to volunteer. You're welcome to join me if you want to."

"I'll probably just sit here and read for a while," I reply, "but when I'm feeling more like my old self, then please ask me again."

She nods and smiles at me, "Just like when you were younger. A comfy chair, a good book and the sunshine. You enjoy that."

21

Until Death, Do Us Part

Tuesday March 5, 2024

Mack

Today is my mom's day off from the diner and I'm planning to spend the day with her. I realize that once I take Lindsey back to Colorado, it will probably be a long time before I'm able to return to Springfield. Mom is, of course, already awake, smoking and drinking coffee, sitting in her recliner.

"Hey. mom. I was thinking with you off and my being home, we could do something today."

"Like, what?" she answers in a very unenthusiastic voice.

I hadn't thought about what we would do, so I just shrugged.

"Well, I need to go to the laundromat so you can tag along."

"Laundromat? Why? What is wrong with your washer and dryer?"

My mom gets up and gestures for me to follow her. I walk behind her to the small laundry room off the kitchen. Both machines are sitting crookedly pulled away from the wall and clearly disconnected. They are the same machines that she has had for as long as I can remember.

"So, the dryer stopped working the day after when your hard-headed brother Brock got arrested the last time. It wasn't that big a deal to hang the wash up to dry, especially since I was the only one living here. So, I didn't bother to get it fixed. Anyway, as you know, Brock spent six months in lock up. The day he came home, he said he could fix the dryer. Somehow, when he was supposed to be fixing the dryer, he fried out the washer. I went to the appliance store, but it is ridiculous what they charge nowadays for stuff, so I've been going to the laundromat."

I shake my head at the mess and say "Mom, let's go to the store and get you a new washer and dryer. I will pay for them."

"You don't have to do that. It's not that big a deal to go to the laundromat."

"Yes, mom it is a big deal and I have the money. Rocky pays me well, so let me do this for you. After all, you took care of me for eighteen plus years."

"I won't turn you down, but we still have to go to the laundromat because I need a clean uniform for tomorrow."

We go to the store and order her new machines, which, per her request, are nothing too fancy. At the laundromat, I notice that not only is she washing her laundry but also Brocks.

"Ma, why are you washing Brock's dirty clothes? He's in his thirties for the love of everything holy."

She shakes her head at me as she continues to load the washing machines. "Listen, when he first came home and broke the washer, I told him that I would do the laundry one week and he would do it the next. Does that seem like an okay way to work it out to you?"

"Yeah, okay, sorry for jumping down your throat." I should have realized that my mom didn't let anyone take advantage of her.

"Well, I thought so until early the Thursday after your dumb ass brothers first week doing the laundry. I went to put my uniform on and he had shrunk it. Not just that one, but all of them. Brock shrunk all my uniforms by putting them in the dryer. So, you see, letting your brother do laundry cost me almost five hundred dollars to replace those uniforms. No, it is better for me to just do all the laundry."

After she finishes loading the laundry into the washer, we walk next door to the hot dog place for lunch.

"Mack, do you know what today is?"

"Tuesday," I answer, wondering where this conversation is going.

"Right, but do you know the date?"

"I think it's the fifth, right?"

"Yes, it is March fifth, which is Chet's birthday. It's the fifth one he is spending in prison. That is hard for a mom. To not be able to bake her kid a cake for his birthday, to not be able to call him and sing happy birthday or buy an actual present."

I never thought about how it felt for my mom that her sons, at least two of them, had turned out so much like their old man.

"Ma, I'm sorry for all that, but you can't blame yourself for other people's choices. Nobody made Chet shoot that store clerk. Anymore then someone made dad shoot the man he did."

She is looking down at the table, picking at her french fries with a plastic fork, so when her voice comes out in a whisper, I have to strain to hear her. "You can't undo choices you make, but I wonder if I would've listened to my folks and stayed in Colorado if Chet would have turned out better."

"I think I misunderstood you because you were whispering, but ma if you would have stayed in Colorado, none of us kids would have been born."

"Chet would have. That is why I ran off with your daddy. I found out I was pregnant and my dad would have gotten Leroy locked up because I was only sixteen and he was twenty-five. So, we ran off together. I just think if Chet would never have been exposed to Leroy, he might be different. Of course, if I had stayed, then you and Brock would never have been born.

I always taught you boys to be loyal to family and to take responsibility for the choices that you make. I don't want you to think that I regret having you or Brock, because I don't. Three hundred sixty-three days a year, I don't think like this, so you just caught me on a bad day."

"Okay, ma I believe you. So, if you think like this on Chet's birthday, what is the other day?"

"The anniversary of the day Leroy and I got married. You know I never divorced him, right?"

"Yeah ma, I know you never divorced him."

"You see, when we first got to Springfield, we stayed with Leroy's aunt and uncle. Somehow, they helped us with the paperwork to say I had parental consent to get married, and so we did. It was at the courthouse in front of a judge, but we took vows, including for better or worse, and until death do us part. I, for one, took those vows seriously."

I nod as mom talks but I don't say anything. Finally, I ask, "So you never even thought about leaving dad and going back to your folks in Colorado?"

"Till death do us part!" is all mom says as she gets up and heads back to the laundromat.

This is one thing that I love most about my mom, her unwavering commitment to her family. That is when it hits me. What I have been doing wrong with Lindsey is that we should have gotten married.

2 2

Trust Your Gut

Wednesday March 6, 2024
Claire

The team is finishing up at the scene of another senior citizen's death at home. Detective Greg Burgeon is in charge of the scene and he isn't a talker, so we don't know much. At first glance, it really looks like Daisy Fletcher died while taking a nap in her recliner. It just bothers me that we are at another unexplained death of an elderly person this week. Sure, it's true that the department investigates all deaths that are unexpected, but for the two years I have been doing this job, I have been at six of these scenes. So, two of them in one week seems excessive.

I share my musing with the team as we drive back to the department.

April replies from the back, "Okay, so I agree. It is sad that these two old ladies died all alone. But I've always thought the best way to go would be in my sleep."

It's not that I disagree with April because, after seeing what some people suffer through before they die, dying in your sleep does seem like the most peaceful way to go. However, that is not what I was getting at.

"Oh, I get that. I guess all I was trying to say was it seems like a strange uptick in elderly women dying in their sleep."

Cal responds, "Honestly, it is a little strange, but neither scene looked violent nor did the deaths. Unless the ME decides that their cause of death was homicide, I think we should just do our jobs and leave the detective work to the detectives."

Dropping the subject seems like the only thing to do in this situation, so I do. At least with my team, the one person I know I can mention it to is Detective Minor. When we are back at the station, I head to see her. Only she isn't at her desk, which I suppose makes sense. I write a quick note asking her to check in with me when she has time and then head to my cubicle on the second floor. I take out the notebook I keep in my desk drawer and write what I know about the death of these two women.

First, I make a t-chart with Hazel on one side and Daisy on the other. Both ladies were in their late eighties, widowed and living alone. Neither of them drove or owned a car. Both of them died in their sleep despite not having a terminal illness or major health condition. There were no signs of forced entry or a struggle in their homes. As I look over my chart, I can see why others don't think there is anything to be investigated. For me, it is just a gut feeling, but as Cal pointed out, I'm not a detective.

Trust your gut that is what my inner voice is saying. Whenever I haven't trusted my gut, I've regretted it. For example, Mack. Years ago, when Lindsey first started bringing Mack around, my gut screamed at me that he was trouble, but I said nothing. As Lindsey changed and distanced herself from me and her parents, my gut told me to tell her that Mack was not the right choice, but I said nothing. When Lindsey came to live with me after Mack broke her wrist and wouldn't talk to me or anyone else about what had been doing, my gut was yelling out again. But once again, I made a choice and didn't interfere with my friend's choices. The time I regret the most is when I saw Lindsey having lunch with Mack days before she took off with him. I asked her about it and she told me to mind my own business. All the while, my gut screamed at me to tell her that he was going to just keep hurting her. My gut wasn't wrong about Mack and I doubt it is wrong about something being off with Hazel and Daisy's deaths.

23

Revelations

Wednesday March 6, 2024

Lindsey

Claire and I are just finishing our dinner of frozen low-calorie meals, and she looks like she is worried about something, probably me. Before Mack, I almost never kept secrets from Claire. But as my life with Mack got more and more complicated, there was less and less, I wanted to share with her. I think that keeping secrets is where I really went wrong. If I turned to Claire, the first time that Mack had belittled me or when he yelled at me or even the first time he hit me, I'm sure she would have helped me.

"Claire, I want to tell you some stuff about what happened with Mack. It will help me if you don't interrupt or ask questions. Do you want me to go on?" I say while I'm washing the few dishes that we used.

"Of course, I want you to trust me to tell me anything that you want. I will sit here quietly."

I purposely don't turn around and face my friend because I don't want to see her reactions. "When Mack and I first got together, he was so good to me and made me feel special and beautiful. So, the first time he got in my face screaming and telling me I was stupid, I was shocked. He made me feel like it was my fault for correcting him about something while we were at my parent's house having dinner. The screaming and name calling began to increase, but I never stood up for myself. I truly believed him that it was my problem. He hit me the first time the night we moved into our apartment together. You had just left, and I decided that unpacking the rest of the boxes could wait. I sat down on the couch next to Mack. He turned and commented on how fast we got everything unpacked. I told him it was only about half done, but I would finish it in the next few days. He slapped me across the face and told me to get up and finish what I had started. I cried while I finished unpacking. What I should have done is leave and come to your house.

One evening right after that, Mack took me out to a nice dinner. He had been so remorseful and apologetic since he slapped me that I had let my guard down. We went to a new Italian restaurant, and the waiter was making jokes and being very attentive. Mack was pissed because he thought we were flirting with each other, but I swear to you we weren't flirting. I was having a great time until I looked over and saw Mack's face. The look he was leveling me sent a cold chill down my spine. I was terrified. When the waiter walked away, Mack stood up and grabbed my hand. We left without ever getting any food. Once we were back at the apartment, he grabbed me by my shoulders and shook me so hard my teeth rattled. Then he pushed me down and before I could get up, he kicked me a few times. I laid there silently crying, and he walked away.

By the time Mack broke my wrist, I wasn't shocked. I'm not even sure if I would have left him then if the neighbor hadn't called the cops and my dad showed up. I was so worn down when I came to live with you that I really did believe that I was the reason that Mack had his outbursts. Looking back on it now, I realize he didn't even have to try that hard to get me to leave Springfield with him. No, he just went back to that loving, charming Mack that I had first fallen for. Of course, that Mack is a lie. He doesn't even exist because we weren't even in Denver a week the first time he screamed at me.

The abuse escalated after about six months. I had learned that if he knocked me to the ground, and I pretended to be unconscious, he would usually walk away. But that time it didn't work, and I really was unconscious; the first time he chained me down in the basement. There were no lights on, no heat, and very little water. It was also the first time that he told me that the only way I was ever leaving him was in a body bag. He reminded me daily from that point on that I belonged to him."

I feel so emotionally drained from dumping all that on Claire that I flop down on a kitchen chair. She is staring at me. "Okay, now you can ask what you want?"

"Why did you stay?"

I shake my head and give a weary sigh, "At first, I thought he was the only man who would ever love me, then later I was crippled with fear."

Claire stands up and hugs me. "That's why you don't want to do your laundry. You are afraid of the basement and the dark because of what you have been through."

"Right. I'm going to work on that fear in therapy. Well, eventually I will. I have a lot to work on in therapy. I think I just needed you to understand that what happened with Mack, it was gradual. It wasn't like we were a perfect couple and one day he just snapped. No, it was more like he conditioned me to take the abuse by slowly escalating it. I'm not telling you any of this to make you feel sorry for me, but because I'm starting to realize that keeping these secrets was only helping Mack and hurting me."

24

Hiding in Plain Sight

Wednesday March 6, 2024
Mack

There aren't many hiding places in a single wide, three-bedroom trailer, but I found one when I was three years old and have used it ever since. In the bedroom's closet, I shared with Brock until Chet went away to prison, there is a floor hatch. The hatch is there so you can get under the trailer for maintenance reasons without removing the trailer's skirting. I would bet money that this one has never been used for that purpose.

I remember the night my dad was on a rampage and I ran to the closet to hide. I sat in that closet for what seemed like hours and I had to pee. I was afraid to leave the closet because I could still hear my dad yelling and I didn't want to pee my pants. So, I was feeling around in the dark for something I could pee into when I felt this little metal ring on the floor. It took a little pulling for it to open. I peered down and saw nothing but darkness, but the need to go overrode my fear of what might be down there, so I jumped down. What I found was the stuff of childhood dreams. A spot of my own that I didn't have to share with my brothers.

At first, I only climbed under the trailer when my dad was screaming, but later, I decided to make the place my own. First, I drug old cardboard boxes down to cover the dirt, then slowly I brought down other things. A rug my mom put in the trash, a battery-operated lantern I found in the shed, and toys. By the time my dad went away to prison when I was almost six, I had made myself a great playroom under the trailer. As an adult, I wonder why no one looked for me, but as a kid, it was nirvana to have a secret spot of my own.

As far as I know, no one has opened the door since I moved out almost four years ago, but when I pull the ring, the door pops right open. I won't be crawling down there, but it has made a great place to store the duffel bag I have my cash in. I put a piece of tape over the edge of the door, when I first put the money down here, that way I will be able to tell if anyone other than me opens it. After checking that the door has not been opened and my money is secure, I head over to a local smoke shop to buy some weed.

It is almost painful to have to pay for the product, but at least it is legal here in Missouri, so I don't have to deal with a street level dealer. If I trusted Brock more, I would suggest opening a smoke shop with him. I could put up the money and he could run it, but somehow, I think this would be disastrous. Plus, once I have Lindsey back, we won't be able to stay in Springfield.

25

Therapy

Thursday March 7, 2024
Lindsey

Looking down at my mom's lap where her hand and mine are clasped together as we wait in the therapist's office, it occurs to me that I haven't grown up. First, I depended on my parents, then on Mack, and now back to depending on my parents and Claire again. I don't know what it will take for me to stand on my own feet, but I'm sure I need to. When I was here on Monday, my new counselor, Becky Price, asked me to think about what I want to accomplish in therapy. Until this very moment, I didn't have an answer for her, but now I know.

Becky calls my name and both mom and I stand up. We hug and mom heads towards the door that leads out of the waiting room while I head towards the door that leads to the offices. Becky makes small talk until we are both seated in her office. Her in her ergonomic office chair and me on the literal and proverbial couch.

"Lindsey, have you thought about what your goal is for therapy?"

Nodding, I reply, "Yes. I want to figure out how to become independent and confident enough for people to stop treating me like an idiot or like I'm a fragile porcelain doll."

Becky, of course, writes something on the pad of paper she always has with her before responding. "Who treats you that way?"

"My parents, Claire, and Mack, all treat me that way." I reply without hesitation. More note scribbling and what appears to be the drawing of four vertical lines proceed, Becky's response.

"Let's talk about each of the people you named individually. Please describe how Claire treats you?"

I don't answer right away because actually Claire has only been treating me like I'm breakable since she rescued me in Denver. Before I ran off with Mack, Claire never treated me that way. "Can we come back to her?"

Becky nods, "Okay, who do you want to start with?"

"Me,"

Looking somewhat startled, Becky urges me to go on.

"I've never been the smartest one in the room nor the prettiest, but I've always been loyal. I think that sense of loyalty makes me too trusting. I have always been very insecure with who I am and I was willing to change to become someone that was appreciated and loved. I spent my school years living vicariously through my best friend, Claire. She is everything that I wished to be. Pretty, smart, good at sports, popular and, of course, petite.

Don't get me wrong, I never tried to compete with her. No, I tried to play to my strengths, which were being funny and outgoing. I wore outrageously bright clothes in elementary school, but in middle school I decided that it would be better to blend in. I wore the typical middle school girl outfit, jeans, band t-shirts and hoodies. I tried to find my place in the social hierarchy, but it was brutal being the fat girl."

Becky looks at me, "Who told you that you were fat?"

Scoffing, I reply "I get it, all you see is this super skinny, likely anorexic chick sitting here, but I was fat. All my life I was a chubby baby, toddler, little kid and teenager. My parents never commented on my weight and they didn't try to put me on a diet or anything, but my mom was always going on and off diets. She has always been really hard on herself about her body, so I think for me it was just always there. You know women are supposed to be a certain size to be attractive or whatever.

Kids at school teased me and I was bullied for being fat. I never had a boyfriend before Mack. When we first got together, he seemed to like me just the way I was. I know now that was a lie, but back then I thought he was attracted to me."

Looking up, I see Becky writing again before she replies. "We will come back to Mack. I think it's essential that we work on you and the way you feel about yourself. In order to help those around you see you differently, you're going to have to start seeing yourself that way."

We spend the rest of the session talking about ways to be kinder to myself and to start to become more independent. Becky encourages me to speak up to my parents and Claire when they overstep, but I'm not ready for that yet. When the session ends, my mom is sitting in the waiting room with a Starbucks cup sitting next to her. She drives me home and offers to do a load of laundry for me. I'm sure Claire has told her that I don't want to go down to the basement. After she starts the washer, we sit on the front porch and talk about her latest cake designs. She shows me pictures on her phone and it is clear how proud she is of the work she does. I want to find something like that. Something I can do really well and be proud of.

She stays long enough to make both of us lunch and finish the load of laundry. After she leaves, I pick the basket of folded laundry up from where it sat between mom and me and walk to my bedroom to put the clothes away. That is when I see it. My bed is made. I know I didn't make it because not making it is an act of freedom from Mack. Not making the bed was a sure-fire way to set him off. He wanted everything in the house to be just so. I'm not sure I will ever make the bed again. I quickly mess the bed up, then sit down and cry.

26

Illusions of Safety

Thursday March 7, 2024
Mack

The girls probably feel safe because the house has security cameras and an alarm system. But it's breaking and entering 1-0-1, that those are easy to get around. Yesterday, I picked up a signal jammer that should knock the signal out to the cameras. I know from my research that as soon as the footage is watched, they will see only fuzz, so I can't use it too often before I go to get what is mine. The jammer will also disarm the alarm system, which is even more risky because the alarm company will quickly be notified that the system has lost the wi-fi connection. The biggest risk, though, is that the jammer is also going to knock out everyone in a thousand-foot radius wi-fi signals. I have to hope that I'm quick enough that no neighbor figures out the issue.

I drive by Claire's house just as Lindsey is getting in her mom's car. This is my chance to try the jammer out and leave a little message for Lindsey. The message has to be clear to Lindsey, but not to others. I don't want her to convince others that I'm stalking her or that I have been in the house. I pull over and put the pest control magnet on the side of the van, push the button on the jammer, pull into the driveway, and park right by the cellar doors. When I walked around at night, I figured out this is my best point of entry. There is a row of tall evergreens between the driveway and the neighbors, so there is no chance of anyone spotting me from that side. There was a simple padlock on the door, so I cut it off, swing the doors open and head inside. I brought another lock with me that looks basically the same, so now I will be the only one with a key. The basement is dark and dank, which I think is a fitting way for Lindsey to spend her last few moments in this house. I spend a little time looking around. There are three bare lightbulbs with chain pulls to operate them. Otherwise, the only light coming in from the two small windows and the cellar door that I left opened.

I head upstairs to the bedroom that Lindsey used to have when she lived here with Claire before. I know immediately it's her room from the smell. Her scent is intoxicating to me, but I don't have time to enjoy it. Shaking my head, I walk over to the bed. I feel the rage building as I quickly make the bed, tucking the sheets and blankets in tight. How many times did I explain to this girl that making your bed every day is a necessary step to having a clean and tidy home? It will be hard for her to miss this reminder of me. I think about picking up the room as well, but decide that I don't have time.

Walking out the cellar steps, I close the door and put the new lock in place. There seems to be no one around, so I quickly get in my van and head down the street. A few houses away, I turn the jammer off. The company said it works from up to a thousand feet away, but I don't want to take a chance on it today. I wish I could see Lindsey's face when she comes into her room and sees the bed. Maybe that is what I need to do next, install a few security cameras of my own. I sit in my van for another twenty minutes, just to be sure the cops or anyone from the security company doesn't show up. When all is quiet, I put the van in gear and head back to mom's trailer.

27

Questions

Thursday March 7, 2024
Claire

This morning has been just like many of my work days are, a monotonous, never-ending pile of paperwork. When I applied, interviewed for and got the supervisor role six months ago, I was so excited. Now I realize that this job sucks. Managing people and paperwork was added on top of all the things that I already did as a CSI tech. Sure, I got a raise, but now it seems like what I really got was the short end of a stick.

I walk to the elevator and head to the Digital Forensics department to see if Abe is free for lunch. A few minutes later, we walk out of the building towards the diner a few blocks away. Abe is telling me about new software that his department is getting and the training that is going to be in St. Louis next month. Only I haven't been listening as my mind wanders to Lindsey.

We have only been back a few days, but already Lindsey seems to be getting stronger. She sits and eats dinner with me each evening and we watch old episodes of Friends. Last night she shared details with me that I wasn't sure she ever would. She is so thin and has fading bruises of all different colors. I want to talk to her more about what happened in Denver, but I don't even know where to start. How do you ask a person you thought you knew so well why she did what she did? I'm afraid that my questions will come off as blaming her. I don't blame her for what Mack did, but I also don't understand why she stayed. After listening to her last night, I am left with more questions than ever.

My parents are divorced, but there was never any violence between them. Not even verbally. As a kid, I struggled to understand why they were splitting up when they never really argued. Since my mom's disappearance and death, my dad has been honest with me about what happened. I have wished many times that I could tell my mom that she did the right thing in divorcing him. When they got divorced, I blamed her and made sure she knew that I thought she broke up my home for no good reason. That was one of the best things about my mom, no matter what was going on, she never trash talked anyone. I remember her telling me that I would understand when I was an adult and me thinking that was bullshit, but once again, she was right.

Lindsey's parents are still married and I've spent enough time there over the last twenty years to say they seem happy. I've heard them argue, but it was never a big thing. Lindsey and I used to joke about the big rocks versus mulch argument of twenty fifteen. Mrs. Peterson wanted Mr. Peterson to rack up all the old mulch around the house and replace it with decorative rocks. Mr. Peterson hated that idea and wanted to just add more mulch. That argument went on for an entire summer until Labor Day weekend. My mom, Mrs. Peterson, Lindsey, and I went away for the long weekend to celebrate Lindsey and me starting high school. When we got back, all the mulch was gone and really pretty decorative rocks had been added.

I guess the point of my musings is that Lindsey grew up around good examples and yet she got caught up in this crap with Mack. Abe touches my arm and says "Earth to Claire."

"Oh sorry, my mind was wandering." I see that we are standing in front of the diner and Abe is smiling down at me. He is almost six feet tall and I am a petite five feet, so he is often smiling down at me. I smile back and let out a little self-deprecating laugh. "Some date I am."

"Oh, this is a date?" Abe chuckles as he opens the door of the diner for me. "I thought it was two colleagues having lunch."

I'm about to respond when I realize he is joking.

Abe continues, "I'm glad it's a date because otherwise my inviting you to join me in St. Louis would be construed as workplace harassment?"

"Join you in St. Louis?"

"Did you hear anything I said on the walk over?"

"Sorry, not really."

Here's the thing about Abe, he is super easy going so it doesn't faze him that I wasn't listening. He just starts over about the software, the training and inviting me to tag along. I'm mindful to stay present in the conversation, so when he invites me this time, I hear him. The thing is, I'm not sure we are ready for a weekend away together. In fact, I'm not sure we will ever be ready for that step.

28

Vigilance

Friday March 8, 2024
Lindsey

I've taken to sitting on the front porch for hours each day. Last night, we changed the settings on the security cameras to continuous recording instead of motion activated. I used the credit card my dad gave me to pay for the service to keep the recordings. It may seem strange, but just knowing that my whereabouts are being recorded gives me a sense of safety. Well, that and the fact that a police cruiser drives by at least every half hour. Sometimes, it is my dad on patrol, but more often than not, it is another officer. I am sure my dad has called in favors at the police department so that he can feel like he is doing something to protect me.

My mom comes by every day. She always brings a treat and a latte but never comments if I don't eat or drink what she brought. Most of the time that she is here, we don't even really talk. I want to ask her about making my bed yesterday and do what Becky suggested about letting her know that while I appreciate the help, I need her to ask me before she does things like that. I don't, of course, say anything to her. It seems ungrateful to tell your mom not to make your bed.

Plus, there is so much that I could say that is more important, but very little that I am ready to say out loud. I'm sure that people think that to be in a relationship where you get abused, you must have come from a bad home, but I didn't. I came from a great one. Several times over the last few days, I have tried to tell my mom just that. Except that I never say the words out loud to her. They seem to be stuck somewhere between my head and mouth like a giant, impenetrable lump in my throat. How can you ever adequately thank your mom for all she has done for you? Especially when you ran off with an abusive man who she tried to warn you about.

Mom left after sitting with me for almost an hour and Claire will be home in a few hours. I've been bringing the same book out with me all week, but not really even trying to read it. The book is a prop because sitting outside reading is a socially acceptable activity. What I really do is much less so, and some would question my mental stableness. I go back to watching the recorded footage for the last twenty-four hours. I put the video at four times speed until there is movement. Watching twenty fours of footage takes an average of nine hours of my day, but the peace that it provides me is indescribable. This weekend I am going to ask Claire about adding some spot lights outside because there have been several times in the middle of the night when there is something in the yard, but because of the darkness, I have no idea what it is.

I take out my notebook and flip to the page I have been using for recording cars that pass by the house. I have added colored tabs for the sections I've made in the notebook. I now know what several of the neighbors drive and their patterns, such as Tom Melnick, across the street. Each morning between 6:41 and 6:46, his garage door opens, and he pulls out in his late model dark blue Honda Civic and drives off to the east. He returns almost every day between 3:31 and 3:35 in the afternoon and rarely leaves again. This is the level of detail I am trying to achieve for all the neighborhood. I figure if I can know the patterns, then I can more quickly spot the anomalies.

Asking my dad for help has crossed my mind a few times, but I don't want him to think I have lost it. I flip to the page that starts the information on vehicles I could not match with owners in the neighborhood. There is one that appears over and over, a blue work van. There are no logos or other distinguishing marks on the van, but there are no windows on the sides or back. I haven't been able to get a clear view of the driver, but there is something about them that has me on high alert. The van seems to have a temporary tag taped where the license plate belongs, but I haven't been able to read it from the camera angles. As I watch the footage, the van passes by four more times and the strangest part is that three of the four times it comes from the same direction, so it's not like they are coming and going from the same location such as their house.

As I watch the footage, I see that van slow down by my house one time and then two other unidentified cars that I'm pretty sure are gig drivers making deliveries. I write down their information on the unidentified vehicles page, which has a yellow tab, and then go back and add the times and directions for all the neighbors' cars that have passed by. I'm sure many people would think the detail to which I'm writing all the comings and goings down is over the top. But when you have lived in a position where you have no say or control over what is happening, being able to decide what you are going to do is liberating. This is what I'm sure my counselor will want me to think about, and I felt better when I focus on the positive and keep my mind busy, but that is not always easy.

29

⧼⧽

Misdirects and Manipulation

Friday March 8, 2024
Mack

I drive slowly past the house and stare at Lindsey sitting on the porch, intently watching something on the laptop screen. She seems to sit there all day long, which I appreciate. I've also noticed the abundance of police cars that are in the neighborhood, which I am sure is her dad's doing. In case I get pulled over, I have put my brother's old toolbox in the back of the van and a clipboard with fake job orders on the passenger seat. I drive by the front of the house four or five times a day and drive the entire block and surrounding blocks each time I drive by. I've found a magnificent spot to park the van at night, just two streets away and a way to access the backyard of Claire's house with minimal exposure. The house has security cameras all around it, but the backyard is pitch dark at night, so it is highly doubtful the girls know I have been back there the past three nights. After watching Lindsey the past few days, I have figured out that I need to break into the house early in the morning after Claire leaves for work. I

93

would have liked to grab Lindsey under the cover of darkness, but Claire seems to stay home most evenings and is never gone at night.

I have two more things to do before I can put my plan into action. The first is to finish figuring out Claire's schedule. When Lindsey and I moved to Colorado, Claire was still in college, so I'm learning what her work schedule is. Actually, I'm not even sure what she is doing these days for work, but that really doesn't matter to me. Claire is inconsequential to me. Yes, she assisted Lindsey in this little escapade, but after I have dealt with Lindsey, Claire will never interfere again. I will make sure that I've delivered the message that Claire is directly responsible for the consequences that Lindsey is about to receive.

Preparing the van is another thing that I have to complete before picking up Lindsey. After leaving her neighborhood, my next stop is at the pet store. When you shop at a pet store buying a kennel, shock collar, and a leash you don't get even a questioning glance from the clerk. When I get back to the trailer, neither my mom nor Brock are there. So, I get right to work. I drag out Chet's welder from the shed and pull it into the back of the van. That shed is a plethora of stuff my dad and Chet have left behind. Including all the things my dad had used for his fake pest control business. That's where I'd gotten the magnet for the side of my van and the stuff that I put in the van in case anyone asked questions. My dad ran the pest control business as a scam to get into people's houses to case them for years. He was committing one of these robberies when the home owner came back unexpectedly and dear old dad shot him at point blank range.

Hopefully, I can finish up this part of my project before anyone comes back. It would be difficult to explain why I am welding a metal dog cage into the back of the van I just bought. Although there is a clip system for the cage already in the van, I'm not taking any chances that it will come loose. It's been a long time since I welded, but it comes back to me once I get started. The welds aren't pretty, but they will hold.

There will be no stops on the way back home, so I need to load up on gas cans, food and beverages, but all of that will have to wait until I put this plan into motion. The next thing that I need to do is create privacy and security in the back of the van. I head into the trailer, grab a beer, and sit down on the couch. A quick search of adding privacy to the back of a van results in many different ways I can achieve what I want. I spend the next hour watching videos and reading tutorials. By the time Brock comes through the door, I have made a list of things I need to buy tomorrow and have a plan for the last part of my van conversion.

"Why do you look like the cat that ate the canary?" Brock says when he hands me a fresh beer and sits down.

I can't see my face, but based on how I feel, I'm sure that it is an appropriate description. I have no intention of telling Brock what I'm planning, but a simple explanation followed by a change of subject should do the trick with my brother.

"I am working on a plan to take care of a problem I've been dealing with and the plan is coming together. It is kind of like when Bill Walsh pulled Joe Montana and put Steve Young in that playoff game against the Vikings." Just like that, Brock is off talking about how the great Joe Montana was the greatest quarterback of all times and he has completely forgotten what he was asking me about.

While Brock goes on and on, I make the appropriate comments without having to really listen to what my brother is saying. Because I have used this misdirect so many times, it is like rewatching a favorite movie.

I think back on some of my favorite times, of misdirecting Brock. Like the time he was a senior in high school and I was a sophomore. He invited a hot girl over to study because he was into her but hadn't worked up the nerve to ask her on an actual date. She was sitting at the kitchen table with books open and my brother was nowhere in sight. I bent down, told her she was hot, and kissed her. That was the moment Brock walked into the kitchen. I took off until later that night and when he was screaming at me, I yell back 'Oh yeah well you are wrong Steve Young was the better choice'. He forgot all about that girl or my kissing her. That is the great thing of knowing someone inside and out. You know the buttons to push to get what you want. I have been able to do it since I was a youngster. Tears worked on my mom but would get me slapped around by my dear old dad. No, with dad, it was best to stay out of sight and make as little noise as possible. That may seem like manipulation to some, but my brothers never got it. They would scream, yell, and run around when dad was in a piss poor mood. It didn't seem to matter how many times they got it from him; they never changed the way they acted.

30

Doubts

Friday March 8, 2024
Claire

I'm at work less than an hour when Detective Minor approaches my desk again.

"Good morning, Claire. Sorry, I didn't follow up with you the other day when you left me a note. I went home sick and spent yesterday completing my yearly re-certification course. What is it you wanted to talk to me about?"

I had spent the last day and half convincing myself that I have been making something out of nothing. Not that Hazel and Daisy's deaths are nothing, but I read that one third of people over the age of eighty die peacefully in their sleep. So, the odds are that these two women are part of this group.

"It's okay, I figured it out."

Detective Minor looks at me like she isn't one hundred percent convinced that I'm being straightforward but moves on. "The ME's office just called me and they have ruled Hazel Green's death to be from natural causes. I reviewed her case with my captain and we have determined that because her children are unsure that there was any money in that box and with no signs of foul play, we are not investigating any further. Sorry for dragging you over there on Tuesday."

What she is saying makes sense to me, and it is not like there is any shortage of work to be done. I nod and respond, "No problem. It's always better to be thorough and have more evidence than we need."

"Agreed. Do you have anything else you need to add to the case file before I close it?"

I tell her that I have processed the evidence that I collected Wednesday and updated my team's report on the Hazel Green case so she can close it.

Abe texted me this morning to ask if I was free for dinner. I told him that I was, and we agreed to meet at six at this great little tapas place. I just need to get through the rest of this work day so I can head home and get ready to go out.

When I arrive home, Lindsey is sitting on the porch with a book open in her lap.

"Hey, how was your day?" she asks as I walk out to the porch with a glass of iced tea.

"Pretty mundane actually, and when you work in crime fighting, that is okay. By the way, I am meeting Abe for dinner tonight?"

"Umm...Abe. Who is Abe, and when can I meet him?"

I chuckle at my friend's response. "Abe is a guy from work who asked me to dinner. Now I need to go get ready for that said dinner."

After showering and picking out what I hope is a pretty dress, but not one that looks like I'm trying too hard, I head to the restaurant. Abe had offered to pick me up, but I prefer to drive myself.

He is already at the restaurant, sitting on a bench by the door. He stands up as I walk towards him, "You look beautiful tonight. Well, of course you look beautiful all the time, but well, you know..."

I hug him and reply, "Thank you, Abe, I know what you mean."

We are seated right away thanks to Abe having made a reservation and both order a drink. We quickly agree to get the sampler for two and place the order when the waiter returns with our drinks.

We talk casually about work, some bands we both like and whether a popular television show has gone too far in the story line to continue to suspend our disbelief. After we have almost polished off the food, Abe asks, "So, about my question yesterday. I didn't mean to freak you out or pressure you or anything. We can get separate hotel rooms. My treat. I just thought it would be nice to spend some time getting to know each other better. I apologize if you thought I was being presumptuous."

I had been wondering if he was going to bring up his invitation to St. Louis again, so I'm prepared with my answer.

"Abe, I don't want to hurt your feelings and please know that I'm not saying that I don't want to date you. It's just that after what happened with my mom, I have trouble trusting people and I'm not sure how to work through that. I'm the one who should be sorry. Is it alright if I think about the trip some more?"

"Of course, it's alright for you to think about it and please don't apologize. Claire, there are things you don't know about me, but believe me that I understand having trust issues and being afraid of getting hurt."

Now Abe has piqued my interest. Is he going to leave me hanging about these things I don't know about him, or will he be elaborating? He is silently pushing a part of a mini-taco around his plate, so I decide to prompt him. "Abe, I would love to know you better. If you're comfortable, I'd like to hear more of your back story."

He looks up at me and says, "Alright but this may seem like a movie or tv show and I really wish it was. I'm adopted. I've known that my whole life. My parents are loving and devoted, so being adopted isn't the issue for me. You see, I was almost five when the Carvers adopted me. I had lived with my birth parents until a few days before I went to the Carvers' house. My dad killed my mom, and I was put up for adoption. I don't have a lot of memories of either of my birth parents and none of the day that my mom died, but there is a void there. A deep desire to understand what happened and a longing to talk to my birth mom. Despite your being older when your mom was killed, you're probably one of the few people who can actually understand that."

I know I'm staring at him, but nothing could have prepared me for what he just told me. The children of the murdered mother's club is a pretty exclusive one, and it seems like fate that I'd ended up dating another member. "Wow. I had no idea. I'm so sorry about all that. You're right; I understand the deep-rooted desire to just sit and talk with your mom."

The waiter returns with the bill at that moment and breaks the spell of our deep conversation. After Abe pays the bill, we walk out to the parking lot and hug one more time.

"Abe, I really will think about St. Louis, and thank you for trusting me enough to share about your mom and dad."

He nods and opens the door to my SUV for me. "Good night, Claire."

31

The Dynamic Duo

Saturday March 9, 2024
Claire

This is my teams on call weekend, which means we will for sure be called in. Crime doesn't care that I would love a day off, so I get up at my regular time, and go through my normal work day morning routine. An hour later, I am sitting in my favorite chair in the living room drinking coffee and reading a trashy chick lit book when Lindsey wanders by. She pauses and says, "Are you working today?".

"Good morning to you, too." I say in a half joking way, "I'm on call and we always get called in on the weekend, so I find it easier to just be ready to go. What are you planning for today?"

Lindsey looks at me with a blank stare before walking away towards the kitchen. She returns a few minutes later with a cup of coffee and sits down on the couch. "Do you know how long it has been since I had a Saturday that I can decide what to do, or for that matter, any day of the week? To answer your question, I will probably sit on the front porch enjoying the sunshine like I have been all week. I have something to ask you."

"Sure, what's up?"

"So, I have been watching some of the footage from the security cameras."

She pauses after saying that and I wonder what she has seen and how worried I need to be. Before I can respond, Lindsey continues.

"Anyway, sometimes in the middle of the night, there is some movement in the backyard. But, I'm not..."

"WAIT, what kind of movement?" I interrupt because now my heart is racing. She has told me repeatedly that Mack is dangerous. Not to mention both of her parents telling me they are worried about his propensity for violence.

Lindsey sighs, "If you would have let me finish, I was going to say it is too dark back there for me to make out what it is. It is probably a dog or something, but that is what I wanted to ask about. Would it be okay with you if I asked my dad to install some motion lights back there?"

My heart is still beating rapidly and the logical part of my brain knows Lindsey is right that it is probably just a stray in the backyard at night. Though that does nothing to calm the panic I am feeling. I nod my head and reply, "Absolutely. Tell him I will pay for the lights."

Lindsey starts laughing, "You know my dad will never let you pay for the lights, but I will tell him you offered. I can tell you are worried and I won't lie and say I'm not. I'm sorry to have put you in this danger."

"Please, don't apologize. None of this is your fault. One thing we have learned since my mom's kidnapping and murder is that she was being stalked. That is why she had the security cameras put in, but she didn't go to the police. I think that she wasn't sure what was going on, or maybe she didn't want to bother anyone. When I was in therapy, I learned to try not to think what if, but I can't help wondering if my mom had trusted her gut would she be here today. So, please trust your gut."

Lindsey stands up and walks the few steps over to the recliner I am sitting in. She sits down on the arm of the chair and lays her head on me. We used to sit like this when we were little. I reach up and pat her on the back. She is crying and now I am too.

"Claire, I'm so sorry for everything that you have been through. I'm so glad you are my friend. Not many people can say they have had the same best friend since first grade."

"You mean kindergarten. We have been best friends since kindergarten. I clearly remember when you moved in and how excited I was when we saw that we were in the same class."

"Okay, sure we have known each other since kindergarten, but we really didn't become friends until first grade. Don't you remember when you kicked that horrible bully for me?"

"Oh yeah, Gibby Johnson. I remember him now. I wonder what happened to him, but we were friends before that."

"Claire, maybe you thought we were friends, but I didn't. I kind of couldn't stand you in kindergarten."

"What? Why? And why am I just hearing about this now?" It irks me that Lindsey is chuckling, but at the same time, it is so good to hear her laugh.

"Okay, okay, don't make a big deal out of it because it was like twenty years ago. The way I remember it was that I thought you were perfect. You were so little, pretty and smart. If you think back, I was already chubby in kindergarten. My mom always called it baby fat, but come on until very recently, I was the chubby friend."

"I never thought of you as the chubby friend. I mean, what were you, a size eight? Maybe a ten in high school? Not that it matters, because what I remember thinking was how cool you were."

"Well, anyway, in first grade, that boy, Gibby, started picking on me relentlessly. He teased me all the time by calling me stuff like "Lotso Lindsey' and 'Cookie Monster', he pulled my hair, and got other kids to gang up on me. Then came the day that he pushed me down at recess and was kicking dirt all over me. You came running up and told him to stop. He started laughing, turned to try to push you, when you kicked him square in the nuts. He fell to the ground screaming, while you reached down and pulled me up. Holding my hand, you ran up to the teacher and said Gibby had been hurting us and you kicked him in the leg so we could get away. I was covered in dirt with tear stains running down my face and one pigtail pulled out."

"Oh yeah, that teacher took us into the office and by the time Gibby got in there, no one wanted to hear his version and how I kicked him in the junk, not the leg."

"After that, no one messed with either of us for the rest of our time at Lincoln elementary school."

"That is the day we became the Dynamic Duo." Now we are both laughing and I decide it doesn't matter if we became best friends in kindergarten or in first grade because we are still friends and few people can say that.

Lindsey changes the subject by asking, "So tell me about your job. Is it like a real live version of CSI, you know, the TV show we used to watch?"

Chuckling, I shake my head, "Yes and no. I mean, I lead a team of other CSI techs, we go out to crime scenes and gather evidence, but it is no way as sensational as the show. Most of the time, it is pretty much taking pictures and dusting for fingerprints. There is so much paperwork. I've never been in a dangerous situation, there are no crazy car chases or sensational love affairs."

Now both Lindsey and I are laughing again. She follows up with, "Speaking of which, tell me more about Abe. You were very evasive last night?"

"Well...I've been seeing Abe for about six months. I'm not sure if he is a special man or a love affair, but we have been getting to know each other. He is really smart, patient and sweet."

Lindsey is looking at me and says, "But?"

"But, what?"

"Claire, I can hear it in your voice. There is a but."

"He works in the Digital Forensics department."

Lindsey looks confused, "Okay, what is wrong with that? You don't like computer geeks?"

"No, it's not that. He is the one who listened to and digitized all of my mom's tapes."

"Her tapes to you when she was being held in captivity?"

"Yes, those tapes. It seems so intimate, but I'm not sure how I really feel about it. He invited me to go away for the weekend to St. Louis when he goes for training and I haven't answered him. I'm not sure I'm ready to take that step with him."

"I would offer you relationship advice, but we both know that would suck."

3 2

Spotlight

Saturday March 9, 2024
Lindsey

Claire got a text message a few minutes ago from work, so she is on her way out. I text my dad about the spotlights and he writes back immediately that he will come by and see what needs to be done. I grab my laptop, notebook and book and take my now regular spot on the porch to wait for him. Less than ten minutes later, both my parents come walking up the front steps.

"So, what's this about needing spot lights?" my dad asks as they both sit down.

I probably should have thought through asking my dad to help. He is going to want to know everything and ask a lot of questions. It is time to show him what I have found.

"Okay, you know that Claire's mom had security cameras installed, right?"

Both of my parents' nod so I continue, "On Sunday, I asked Claire to have them start recording continually instead of just for motion. I sit out here every day and watch the footage."

At that point, I hand my dad my notebook and watch as he opens it. He skims through the pages and says, "You would make a good detective. Tell me about this blue van."

"Everything I know is in there. Mack has a black truck, so I'm pretty sure it isn't him. The thing is, look at the page with the red tab. That is where I have written about things at night in the backyard that I can't make out what they are. The motion sensor lights are, so we know what or who is back there."

My dad is looking at the pages I mentioned and then says, "Let's go look in the back so I can figure out the best place to put lights on and what else I need to pick up to install them. While we head to the hardware store, you can tell me more about your sleuthing and why you didn't ask for help immediately."

I sigh but know that dad really does have my best interest at heart. I'm sure he wonders where he went wrong with me. How does the daughter of a cop end up in a situation like mine? That's one question that I just have to hope he won't ask me because I have no suitable answer.

As dad and I head to the back of the house, mom leaves to go to work. She has put the finishing touches on a wedding cake for this evening and worked on a few other orders. She hugs me before she leaves and whispers, "Remember, your dad is just worried about you. Don't get upset with him for being nosy."

I nod my head at her in response and watch her walk back towards their house. Dad walks all around the backyard and then the sides of the house as well, with me trailing him like a puppy. A very silent puppy. He is writing things down in his little flip notebook that he always has with him. I asked him once when I was little about his notebooks and he said that "a good cop knows the importance of keeping accurate notes". The comment didn't make a lot of sense to me as a kid, but now that I'm writing detailed notes about the camera footage, I'm beginning to see how it is helpful.

As we approach the front of the house again, dad tells me he is going to go grab his truck and come back to get me. He looks like he wants to hug me but is afraid I'll break. Instead, he waves and says, "Be ready in five minutes."

I go through the house and make sure all the doors are locked, then set the security system to away. Dad is pulling up just as I walk back outside. I get in the passenger seat and try to steel myself for the barrage of questions.

"What can I do to help you, Lindsey?"

"Daddy, you are helping me right now. I'm probably being paranoid, but the lights will help me feel safer."

"I talked with a detective at work and she said that if you want, she would sit down with you so you can tell her what happened in Denver. Then she can help you decide if you should file a police report there. I figured you would be more comfortable with a woman, and Detective Minor is one of the best detectives the department has."

I'm not sure what to say at first. "Okay, thanks dad. I'll think about it, but I think if Mack stays away from me that I just want to be done with him and start putting it behind me."

"If that piece of shit shows up here, he is going to regret it."

"I know you hate him, dad but don't do anything that you'll regret. If he shows up, I'll call for help and this time I will press charges. I promise."

My dad's knuckles are white where he is gripping the steering wheel, and he nods ever so slightly. He is a natural protector, so I'm sure it is killing him to know that he didn't protect me. "Dad, what happened with Mack, it wasn't your fault. You and mom are great parents. I just fell for the wrong guy and was in too deep when it got really bad. My counselor has already talked to me about how many women go back to their abusers, but I promise that will not happen this time."

Dad pulls into a parking spot at the large home improvement store, puts the truck in park, and turns to look straight at me. "Lindsey, I know you don't want to share the details and that is your decision, but

I've been a cop for almost thirty years. That means I have seen a lot of domestic abuse cases and what the victims look like. I know Mack beat and starved you. What I don't know is why you didn't come home the first time it happened in Denver. I'm not asking you to answer that, but I want you to know that you can always call me and I'll come and get you, no matter where you are or what has happened."

He has tears in his eyes and I'm straight up, crying my eyes out. I release my seatbelt and scoot over to him. He engulfs me in a hug and it hits me that this is what real love feels like. It feels like safety!

33

Thanks for the Gun Dad

Saturday March 9, 2024

Mack

I stop at the corner just as Lindsey's dad passes by and I can clearly see her in the passenger seat. I feel like everything has been going in my favor since I arrived back in Springfield. I was planning to do my morning drive by twenty minutes ago but was running late. If I would have been on time, there is a good chance Mr. Peterson would have spotted me.

This morning, I had to wait for Brock to leave so I could dig up dad's old gun. When dad got jammed up, the police searched high and low for the gun. But my dad outsmarted them by burying it behind the trailer. I know exactly where it was because he made me dig the hole. I dug while he put the gun and ammo in a bucket with a lid, then dug up one of mom's peonies from the front yard. When we were done, dad sprinkled dead leaves and grass across the top. No one ever asked why there was one lone flower bush in the backyard.

After I dug up the bucket, I took out the gun and ammo, then put the bucket back in the ground, covered it with dirt once again and

110

replanted the bush. My dad kept this gun in meticulous shape and taught all of us boys how to clean it when we were still little. I set the gun on my bed and grab the cleaning kit out of the front hall closet. After cleaning the gun thoroughly, I load it and head to the woods where dad taught us to shoot. The gun fires with no issues and my aim is still decent.

I park the van at the corner and casually walk towards Claire's house with a small package tucked under my arm. I switch on the jammer a few houses away. I don't know how long Lindsey and her dad will be gone, so I pick up my pace as I walk down the driveway to the cellar door. When I open the door at the top of the basement steps, one of their stupid cats runs by me. I have never understood why people let animals live in their houses. Opening the door to Lindsey's room, I am astonished by the mess. How could she be living like this? I trained her better than this.

The first thing I do is open the package I brought with me and pull out the teddy bear. It is one of those nanny cam type stuffed animals. When I was here Thursday, I saw that there was a small grouping of stuffed animals in a chair in the corner. I'm hoping this little gift of mine blends in and goes unnoticed. I position the bear the best that I can because I can't check the feed of the camera because of the jammer. If the positioning doesn't give me the view I want, I will just come back and move it.

Then I begin picking up dirty laundry and throwing it in the empty hamper. I grab a pair of panties and can't resist the temptation to sniff them. Lindsey's scent has always been intoxicating to me. The anger begins to bubble up as I think about all I have done for her and that she ran away like she did. We are soul mates and I thought she knew that. The love I feel for her isn't ever going to end and neither will our relationship. I am thinking about how to get Lindsey to truly understand our bond when I hear the sound of a vehicle. Carefully, I pull back the curtains and sure enough, Lindsey and her dad are pulling up to the curb. I shove the panties into my jean pocket and race through the house to the basement.

Ascending the cellar door stairs, I carefully look around but see no one. Then I hear her melodic voice drifting towards me from the front.

"Dad, I doubt Claire has a ten-foot ladder. Just go home and get yours. I will carry all this stuff to the back of the house."

So, with no time to waste, I close the cellar door, replace the lock, race towards the back of the house and slide between the fence and garage. I unjam the camera system and wonder how I'm going to get out of here without being seen. I peer through the window on this side of the garage and can see straight through the window on the other side and into the backyard. Lindsey walks right by without looking over at the garage. She is carrying several bags from a large home improvement store. I wonder what she and her dad are up to.

The next load she lugs back answers the question. She has three boxes that are labeled *motion activated outdoor spotlights*. Interesting. Someone must have seen my movements back here at night. I don't see any other way to leave but to go through the backyard and into the neighbor's yard. Hopefully, they aren't home because having the cops called on me for trespassing would put a major dent in my plans.

<h1 style="text-align:center">34</h1>

Family Secrets

Saturday March 9, 2024
Claire

This morning's crime scene had started out as a multi-vehicle accident that would normally not have gotten the on-call CSI team sent out. That is until one of the drivers took off running from the scene. The responding officer called in the plates and that is when he realized that the car was stolen. So, there we were on a lovely Saturday, on the side of the road dusting a car for prints and taking swabs for possible DNA. Again, out of the norm because generally this would have been done in the evidence garage, but as fate would have it, the police department's tow truck broke down and it is going to be hours before a private rig can take care of it.

It only took my team about an hour and a half to finish the evidence collection, and Cal volunteered to take everything back to the station. He said he was willing to process the evidence as well, and none of us objected. I know his wedding is coming up in a few months and he is trying to bank all the comp time he can to use for the time off. Before heading home, I headed to the grocery store, which should have been a relatively quick errand but turned into an hour plus trip because of my dad's wife, Dawn. She was at the store and she is a talker. Luckily for me, there is a Starbucks right in that grocery store, so I suggested we grab a coffee and a seat.

"So, tell me about this impromptu trip to Denver? Your dad was concerned that you went alone."

I suppress my sigh because I know my dad cares about me, but sometimes his worry seems over the top. "How much did he tell you about Lindsey?"

Dawn shrugs, "You know your dad. Details are not his strong suit, so how about you start at the beginning?"

She is, of course right, details are not one of my dad's strengths. "Lindsey and I have been friends since kindergarten. We were practically inseparable throughout our school years. She is like my sister and spent as much time at my house as I did at hers. In a lot of ways, we are opposites, like she is tall with dark hair and beautiful brown eyes as opposed to my pale skin, red hair, and green eyes. As you know, I love physical activity and played sports in high school and college whereas Lindsey well to hear her tell it, she hates sweat."

Dawn chuckles a little at that comment as I continue. "She was my rock when mom disappeared. Then I went off to college, and she met a guy. His name is Mack, and I never liked him. I knew better than to tell her that, but he was controlling of her from the very beginning of their relationship. About three years ago, they had a fight, and he broke her wrist and she left him. She lived with me for almost eight months, then she left me a note that she and Mack were leaving and not to bother them. She also left her parents a very similar note.

Her dad is a cop, and he talked with a detective about Lindsey but pretty much was told that she is an adult and can go where she wants with whomever she wants. Neither her parents nor I had heard from her in almost two years when I got a message from her at the end of February."

"What kind of message did you get from her?" Dawn asks.

"It was an envelope with my name and address on it. Inside was a torn off scrap of paper with the words *"Large Pineapple Anchovy pizza* on one side of it and an address in Denver on the other."

Dawn looks perplexed, but before she can ask a question, I continue. "That was a

code our moms came up with when we were little, so we would know if someone was safe for us to go with. Lindsey and I used it later to let each other know when we were not feeling safe and wanted to leave some place. So, you see, when I saw the paper, I knew Lindsey needed me. I thought about telling her parents, but I didn't want to get their hopes up, so I just drove to Denver."

"Okay, I get that, but why not ask your dad and I to come with you?"

"And, say what? Would you two go on a road trip to what may or may not be my

friend Lindsey's place? Because she may or may not have sent me a cryptic message that she needs to get out. I get why dad was worried. The other thing is I really didn't think I was in danger. I figured Lindsey needed a ride, not that Mack was holding her prisoner. I thought I would drive to Denver, Lindsey would hop in my SUV, and we would drive home. I was naïve to not think about how bad it might have gotten, but we are back safe and now we just need it to stay that way."

Dawn leveled a glare at me that said she didn't want to drop the subject of my driving to Denver alone that quickly. However, she did move on and ask me, "Did your dad ever mention that I had a sister?"

I shake my head, "I thought you just had the one twin brother that you own the auto

shop with."

"I don't talk about Eve much because it is so hard. She was murdered twenty

years ago, by her husband."

I audibly gasp and wonder why Dawn is sharing this with me. Before I can ask she continues her story.

"Eve was the baby of the family; Gary and I were in high school when she was born. I remember my mom thought she was in menopause, then she found out she was pregnant again. Both of us had moved out by the time Eve started school and so we weren't ever close. She started dating Jeff when she was sixteen and he was twenty. Jeff, that's her scumbag husband's name. They got married right after she graduated from high school and their son, Leon, was born about a year later.

I was busy with my life, and she was busy with hers. Plus, we had never been that close, so I can't say I'm shocked that she never came to me when the abuse started. But I can say I'm pissed that she didn't. I would have gotten her and Leon out of there faster than a 1969 Pontiac GTO pulls off the line. What I do know is that Eve went home to our parents with Leon on at least three separate occasions before the night she died. But every time Jeff came around and somehow talked her into coming back. I also know my dad regretted not stopping her until the day he died.

I don't know exactly what is going on with your friend Lindsey, but I do know that

these abusive guys don't stop until they get what they want. Do you know if this POS boyfriend of hers is back in town?"

I tell her that we don't know for sure where Mack is and that Lindsey and I are

being careful.

"Do you carry a gun for work?" Dawn asks.

"No, I'm considered a civilian employee, not a law enforcement officer, why?"

"I think that if you don't already know how to, that you and Lindsey need to learn to shoot a gun. I'm sure her dad or someone you work with can take you to the shooting range, or I will. Then, when you're both comfortable, we will buy each of you one."

"Dawn, I appreciate where you're coming from, but having guns in the house seems like a bad idea to me."

She shakes her head, "No honey, having a crazed, abusive ex is a bad idea. So, if no guns, how about a dog? A large, protective one."

"I guess we could get a dog as long as it likes cats. Thanks for the suggestion." Talking with Dawn and hearing about her sister has drained all my emotional energy. "I better get the groceries and head home. I don't want Lindsey to start worrying about me."

Dawn nods and stands when I do. "Call anytime and tell Lindsey to come on by

the shop when she is ready, and I will give her a job at the front desk."

"Thanks, I appreciate that and I'm sure she will too." Dawn doesn't try to

hug me, which is a relief because I would have started sobbing. I know technically she is my stepmom, but she has never tried to be a mother figure to me and I appreciate that. I remember not being sure about her when my dad first introduced us. She is fifteen years older than him, tattooed and muscular, but they seem happy. I'm happy that my dad got a second chance at love.

35

Old Friends, New Tricks

Saturday March 9, 2024
Lindsey

Dad and I worked the rest of the day putting up the spotlights on the back of the house and various other improvements he felt were necessary. Claire had come home with groceries just as we finished the lights, so dad had asked her about the other things he wanted to do. After they talked, he and I went back to the hardware store for supplies. He bought metal plates for the front and back door jams, two new deadbolts, and two door blocking locks. He had me hand him tools and parts as he made both the doors of the house more secure. Then he showed Claire and me how to engage the door blocking locks that were now on the base of the front and back doors.

I wander into the kitchen after hugging my dad on the front porch and saying thank you and goodbye. Claire is at the stove cooking something that smells delicious.

"What are you making, and when did you learn to cook?"

"Chicken stir-fry and I've been teaching myself to make things for the last couple of years. This is one dish I have gotten really good at. Will you please put the egg rolls into the air fryer?"

"Sure, I can still warm things up.", I reply with a chuckle.

A few minutes later, I take my first bite of the meal Claire made and audibly groan, "OMG, Claire, this is so delicious." I eat an entire small serving of the stir-fry, noodles and an egg roll. All that food makes me feel overly full but so satisfied at the same time. I realize that it has been years since I really enjoyed food without worrying about the calories, carbs and fats that it contained.

"I'm glad you liked it. I would be happy to teach you to make it sometime." Claire says as I begin to clear the dishes off the table.

"It was divine, but I'm not sure I will ever want to learn to cook." My learning to cook and bake has been an ongoing joke between my mom and me since I was little. With her having superior kitchen skills and me having no interest in learning.

"No problem, I just thought I'd offer. Did I mention that I ran into Dawn at the grocery store today?"

I shake my head and ask, "How is she?"

"Same as always. I only mentioned it because she told me that if you are looking for a job, she needs someone at the front counter of the auto shop."

A job, now there is something I do need, but I wonder how I will get there every day since I don't have a car. "Do you know if the shop is near a bus line?"

Claire looks confused at first but quickly recovers and tells me she doesn't but is sure we can figure it out before I decide if I want to apply.

We spent the evening watching *Friends*. Five years ago, for Christmas, I gave Claire the ten season DVD box set of our favorite tv show. Watching the episodes brings back happy memories and I'm sure that is why she chose this for us to watch. Claire seems distracted and thinking about something else during the episodes. Despite being curious about what is going on with her, I don't ask. Mostly because I'm afraid that it is about me, or Mack, or both of us, and I'm not ready to talk to her about any more of it yet. I just hope she doesn't want me to move out because she fears for her safety.

36

Watching and Waiting

Saturday March 9, 2024

Mack

I pull my van into a back parking spot of the nearby grocery store and open the app for the nanny cam. Fate is once again on my side as the positioning of the bear couldn't be better. I have a clear shot of the bed that Lindsey sleeps in. I know I'm going to be checking the live feed continuously this evening, so I don't miss seeing her going to bed tonight. I confirm the settings of the app are to notify for any movement and then tuck my phone into my pants pocket.

Now it's time to shop for supplies. I load my cart with drinks, food and snacks for our upcoming road trip home. I'm sure Lindsey hasn't been keeping up with her diet this week, so I stick to low calorie choices for her. Sometimes I wonder if she remembers how miserable she was when she was fat and I first met her. I could tell immediately that she had the right bone structure, that with proper discipline, could be shaped into a great figure. It still amazes me how she used to eat, but I suppose she didn't know better since her mom is overweight, too.

I'm walking out of the produce section when I hear someone say my name. As I turn to look, I see my old pal Ben heading towards me. He has three little kids in a cart and no woman in sight.

"Hey buddy, how's it going? I thought you moved away?" he says as he approaches.

"Going good, and Lindsey and I did indeed move away. We are just home visiting. Actually, I'm here stocking up for our drive home." I point to his cart full of rugrats and ask, "Are they all yours?"

Ben laughs, "Yep and all boys. This is my weekend with them and, like usual, I'm too stupid to do the grocery shopping before I get them from their moms."

I'm not sure if he means their mom's place or if they have multiple moms. "Oh, wow! Three kids in the three years since I last saw you, that was quick."

"Well, yeah, but they each have a different mom, so they are only about six months apart from each other. Casper is the oldest and he will be three this June, Temor was two in January and Rubio will be two in July."

I try to keep the judgement I feel out of my voice, "Okay man, I just gotta ask, did you forget all that stuff we learned in sex ed?"

"Now you sound like my dad. He's always giving me a hard time about these three. Especially since I moved back in with my folks because paying three chicks child support leaves me broke as an old Ford truck. But no man, I didn't forget, I just got caught up in the heat of the moment. Anyway, these guys are cool and I like being a dad. I take it you and Lindsey got no kids."

Although it is a statement, there is an implied question there. "We are both enjoying our carefree life too much for that. Good to see you, man. I need to get going. Take care of yourself and all these guys."

"Thanks man. It was great to see you. Tell Lindsey I say hi and the next time you're in town, swing by my folks' house to say hi."

I shake his hand, then turn and walk away. I can't imagine having three kids, much less having three kids and not being with their mom.

One day, when we are ready, Lindsey and I will have a couple of kids and I have vowed that they will never have to spend time between two houses or wonder if their dad is coming home. No, part of being a dad for me is having a rock-solid relationship with my woman, so my kids know what a good family is like. That is something I didn't have as a kid. Even before my dad got jammed up and went away for life, he was in and out of the trailer. Which left my mom to be in charge of all three of us boys all the time while working full time and let me tell you that led to problems.

My oldest brother, Chet, was always getting into trouble at school, with the neighbors and the cops. He was five when I was born and I really don't remember a time when he wasn't a hellion. The neighbor next door, Mrs. Cranston, was supposed to be our babysitter while mom was at work and Brock and I would stay with her, but not Chet. From the moment he woke up, he was running around, causing havoc. Mrs. Cranston, who I thought was ninety then but must not have been because she is still alive, didn't even seem to try with him. I remember her telling my mom once that 'Chet is too much like his dad to have anything good happen to him'. That comment must not have bothered mom that much because Mrs. Cranston looked after us until I was eleven.

When my dad would grace us with his presence, he was always drunk and surly. I never knew him to have a straight job and so I'm sure he rarely helped out financially. I asked my mom once why she stayed married to him and kept letting him come back and she said something like 'I made my bed and now I have to lie in it'. Which as a kid made no sense, but now I get that she was talking about her choice to leave Colorado with my dad when her family hated him. I wish Lindsey would show the same kind of loyalty to me.

I take a nap when I get back to the trailer because I'm planning to watch the live feed of Lindsey for a good portion of the night, and why not? It's not like I've got any other place to be. I wake up to the sound of the screen door slamming and Brock talking loudly with some other guy. When I wander out to the living room, Brock is sitting on the couch with a beer in his hand and a big guy is sitting in ma's chair also holding a beer.

"Hey, little brother. This is my friend Brock, but everyone calls him Bud. Bud, this is my brother Mack. The one I was telling you about who lives in Colorado."

The big guy and I nod at each other as I pass by on the way to the kitchen. I open the fridge and ask, "Anybody need another one?" Brock nods and Bud shakes his head. That's when I notice Bud looks like he has been exercising or some crap. He is all sweaty and dirty.

I sit down next to my brother and say, "So Bud, how do you know my brother?"

"Jail."

That one-word answer is all he says.

Brock snickers and adds, "It's funny because we are both named Brock and were in the same cell block. The guards called us Brock Squared."

I turn my gaze to Brock. "Um, isn't a condition of your probation to not hang out with known felons?"

Brock laughs, "Who said Bud was a felon? Nah, he just got jammed up for petty crap like me. Isn't that right, Bud?"

The big man simply nods one time in response.

Brock puts on a rebroadcast of a Chiefs game from last season and the three of us watch it. The only conversation is about the game and the Chiefs. After the game wraps up, my brother and his friend tell me that they are heading out. They leave and I go back to checking the nanny cam application on my phone every fifteen minutes. It is almost nine o'clock when I get alert of movement. I open the app and see the shadow of the door come across the bed on the screen. Lindsey walks right by the camera and takes a pair of sweatpants and a long sleeve shirt out of the dresser then walks back out the door. Twenty minutes later, she is back and is clearly freshly showered with her long hair braided down her back.

She turns on a small light by the bed, turns off the overhead light, climbs into bed, picks up a book that is sitting on the nightstand and reads for about twenty minutes. I can tell when she begins drifting off as her head begins to bob down and then up again. Within minutes, Lindsey sets the book down and turns off the bedside light. The room is too dark for me to see much once the light is off, but I can clearly see her shape in the bed and periodically throughout the night, I watch her sleep.

37

Curiosity and the Cat

Saturday March 9, 2024
Claire

When I get home from the grocery store, I do what any curious person would do. I google the names Eve and Jeff, adding the term murder to the search. Sure enough, there are a bunch of stories from twenty years ago and a more recent one from five years back. I decide to start with the oldest one and work my way to the newest. I read all the articles in between talking with Lindsey and her dad about stuff he wants to do to make the house more secure.

It seems there was never a question of who killed Eve, as Jeff was sitting on the floor of the living room next to her body when the cops arrived. A neighbor had called 911 when they heard Leon crying inside Eve's locked car and neither of his parents coming outside. When the patrol car arrived, they got the little boy out of the car and gave him to the neighbor to watch while the patrol officers went to see what was going on. They found the front door open, several suitcases just inside the door, and what was described later at Jeff's trial as signs of a violent struggle. After identifying themselves, the officers went into the house, where they found Jeff sitting next to Eve on the floor.

Jeff didn't respond when they told him to put his hands up or when they asked him to identify himself. He put up no resistance when the officer cuffed his hands behind his back and walked out to the patrol car in what seemed like a daze. Eve was declared dead at the scene and at the trial, the medical examiner testified that she had been strangled. Eve had defensive wounds and Jeff's skin and blood under her fingernails.

He had some high-priced lawyers who got him out on bail during his trial. They argued the usual, not a flight risk, ties to the community, no criminal history, yadi yada. At the trial, Jeff's defense was temporary insanity, with his lawyers arguing that he lost it when he found Eve preparing to leave him and take their son. The prosecution pointed out the history of visits to the emergency room, the multitude of police calls to the house over the years, and that the only reason Jeff didn't have a criminal history was that Eve refused to admit he hurt her. A chill ran up my spin when I read this. It was hard not to think of Lindsey and how she used to make excuses for Mack.

The day the jury went out to deliberate was the last day anyone set eyes on Jeff. He parked his car at the airport and the police tracked him getting on a flight to Morocco using an alias and a fake passport. Seems Jeff didn't think the verdict was going to come back in his favor. I wondered what one does when they flee to a foreign country. Like did he get a job, get remarried, just start his life over, or was he like a homeless bum? Did he go back to his real name or use the alias for all these years? What did he tell people about why he was there?

The story from five years ago was the newspapers follow up on the fifteen-year anniversary of Eve's murder and, after recapping all the stuff I had already read, it added that Jeff had never returned to the United States. There was no mention of what happened with Leon, and I wondered if I could ask Dawn about him. She had mentioned little about her nephew when she told me the story earlier today. So,

I was guessing he didn't go to her parents or brother to be raised. I knew Dawn didn't raise him because the first I had ever heard of Leon was at the grocery store today.

Something is bothering me, but I can't quite figure it out. I decide to head to the kitchen and start dinner. Hopefully, doing something else will help me figure out what I'm missing. We have been back almost a week and since I worked every day; we have been eating frozen meals. But today I didn't work all day long so, it is a great chance to show Lindsey my recently acquired cooking skills. I have perfected three things: chicken stir-fry, baked ziti, and enchiladas. I always make enough to feed four people and freeze half of the leftovers for quick meals. Tonight, I will make the chicken stir-fry with lo-mien noodles and egg rolls. I buy the mini egg rolls premade but otherwise this is a homemade meal and before Lindsey went to Colorado; she loved Chinese food so I'm hoping it will be a hit.

I'm halfway done making the stir fry when Lindsey comes into the kitchen. She is surprised that I learned to cook but doesn't turn down dinner. She eats like it is the best food she has ever eaten. She is so intent on eating that we don't really talk at all during dinner. After we finish eating, I casually bring up talking with Dawn today and the job offer. I'm planning to lead the conversation to Dawn's sister and what had happened to her, but Lindsey throws me off my train of thought. She asked about the bus routes and I couldn't immediately process why she was asking about them. After my brain kicks back in and I realize she has no car, I tell her we will look up the routes on the internet so she can decide if she wants to apply.

We do the dishes together, then I suggest that we watch some tv. I grab the DVD box set of Friends that Lindsey gave me one year for Christmas and pull out the disc that has season four on it. That is the best season in my opinion. I pop the DVD into the player and settle in on the recliner near Lindsey. I have to admit that I hardly watch the show for two reasons, the first being that I have seen it many times and the second being I just kept thinking about Eve, her murder, Lindsey, Mack and how much it would hurt if Lindsey was killed. The latter being the central reason that I tuned out the show. I'm happy Mr. Peterson installed the motion lights in the back and the other safety precautions he added, but honestly, I'm afraid for Lindsey. I think about the self-defense class my mom took me to all those years ago and wonder if I should suggest that. Then again, it didn't save my mom from being kidnapped and murdered.

As the movie ends, I see Lindsey looking at me, then looking away. I wonder what she is thinking about or if she just could tell I'm preoccupied.

"I'm on call, so I'm going to head to bed just in case I get called in to work again. I will leave you a note if I do and you're still asleep. Otherwise, let's plan to do something fun together tomorrow, okay?"

Lindsey nods, "I would love that. Thank you, Claire, for all you have done for me the last week or so. I love you."

I stand up and walk over to her, we hug and I say, "I love you, too. You're my sister and I will do anything you need me to."

38

Scopaesthesia

Sunday March 10, 2024
Lindsey

After grabbing my stuff, I'm back in my now usual spot on the front porch by eight in the morning. I fast forward the video footage from yesterday to the nighttime. I wrote myself a note to go back and watch the whole day, but for now I want to see how the spotlights worked. My dad had worked for hours to get the lights up and running, and I want to tell him that they worked well. Most of the night is dark and still in the backyard except for one time when a dog wanders through and a couple times when a pack of raccoons scurry around, jumping on and off the garbage and recycling cans.

I send my dad a text:

Lindsey: Thanks again for your help. The lights worked great last night.

Dad: You're welcome, So, what did you see on the footage?

Lindsey: A stray dog and a bunch of racoons. Claire & I are safe even if our trash

isn't ;)

Dad: Good, but don't stop being vigilant about your safety. Love you.

Lindsey: Love you too!

Claire walks out onto the porch just as I set the phone down. "Good morning sleepy head. I didn't expect you to sleep in."

"Yeah, me either, but I had trouble sleeping last night. I figured if work called, I would just get dressed quickly and deal with it. By the way, have you seen Monica this morning?"

I shake my head and ask "Why?"

"I think she must have gotten out yesterday. I know she is a lot less social than Rachel, so I wasn't too worried when she hadn't been around after I got home yesterday. But she almost always sleeps on my bed and didn't last night. I noticed this morning that her food dish is still full from last night."

"Okay, so that is all odd and makes me agree maybe she got out. I just don't know how or when."

"Is it possible your dad left the door open yesterday when he was putting up the lights and fixing stuff?"

"Yeah, I guess so. We never had a pet, so he might not even think about the cat getting out."

"I'm going to leave her food dish out here on the porch and hopefully she'll wander back home. So, do you still want to do something today?"

Whatever was bothering Claire last night seems to have passed and I'm relieved. "Sure. What did you have in mind?"

Claire smiles, "I was thinking we could walk downtown like we did when we were younger. There is a newish bookstore and coffee shop called Books and Brews that I thought we could check out."

"Two things I love; books and coffee, I'm in!"

After Claire puts out Monica's food, we lock up the house and head out. It really does feel like old times, walking arm in arm with my friend on a beautiful spring day. As we walk, Claire tells me about some people we went to high school with, as well as a few funny stories from work. The coffee and book shop is everything I had hoped for and more. We both order drinks and browse the shelves while enjoying them.

The store has both new and used books as well as what can only be described as an eclectic mix of notebooks, stickers, pens and magnets. I'm skimming a book on goal setting when I get the eerie feeling of being watched. Looking around, I don't see anyone staring at me, but as I look out the big front window, I see a shadow of a person walking away. My mind is whirling, *Is that Mack? Is he following us?* I set the book down and head towards the door to see if I can spot who it was.

I'm standing on the sidewalk after doing a full spin to look all around me when Claire walks out.

"You left without telling me. Why?"

I can't seem to find the words to tell her that I think Mack was staring at me. That he is here in Springfield and following us.

"What's wrong? You're shaking and pale as me?" Claire asks as she guides me to a bench.

The tears began to silently slide down my face.

"Take a deep breath. Smell the roses, blow out the candles." she says as she rubs my back in little circles.

"What?"

Claire looks confused, "That is what I want to know. What is wrong?"

"What did you say about flowers and candles?" her words seemed to have broken the fog I was in.

"Oh, it is something I learned in therapy. A breathing technique. You pretend to smell the roses so you take a deep inhale. Then you blow out the candles as a way to completely exhale the breath. It works, just try it."

I do try it, and so does Claire. I'm sure we looked crazy sitting on a bench downtown breathing deeply, but it does help calm me.

"I was looking at a book when I felt someone staring at me, then I saw a shadow of a person walking away from the window. I ran out to see if it was Mack, but whoever it was had already left.

There are people walking past us as I tell Claire this, and she looks at them and gestures her open hand with a sweeping motion.

"Lindsey, there are people walking around down here. Someone may have stopped to look at a book in the window. Why do you think it was, Mack?"

"It is not something I can explain and maybe it is my paranoia, but I just sensed him."

"Do you want to head home? I can call someone to pick us up."

I take a few more deep breaths and shake my head. "Not really. Mack has ruined too much of my life already. I want to enjoy this time with you. What other shops did you want to show me?"

"Great. Let me go in and pay for the book I want, then we will head to this great boutique. Did you find anything you wanted?"

I quickly shake my head again. I'm sure Claire would pay for the book or anything else I picked out, just like she paid for our coffees. But it feels wrong to take advantage of her generosity. I need to get a job. Claire returns in a few minutes, holding a small bag.

"What did you get?" She pulls out a cookbook and smiles.

"My next dish to conquer is going to be fried chicken, and this cookbook has a great sounding recipe and very precise instructions."

We start walking and pop into almost every shop along the way to the boutique, Claire wants to show me. The revitalization of downtown was something being talked about when I moved away and it seems to be working. We walked through a candy shop, a shoe store, and two vintage shops. It is kind of sad to see all the things that used to be important to someone on display for sale. Especially the framed photos and handmade items. Someone's time and money went into those things, but when they were gone, no one in the family wanted them. Or maybe they had no family left to care. My melancholy thoughts are interrupted by Claire walking up holding a doll.

"Do you remember when we both wanted this doll more than anything else for Christmas? We were like eight years old and neither of us got one. I think I'm going to buy her for us now."

I look at the doll and remember that Christmas. My parents were going to buy the doll, but Claire's mom, Kelsey, told my mom that she just couldn't afford it. My mom sat me down and told me that if I really wanted the doll, they would buy it, but that it would probably hurt my friend's feelings. As much as I wanted that doll, I didn't want Claire to be sad, so I told my parents not to get the doll. I don't say any of that to Claire and instead say, "Cool. Do they have any of the accessories?"

We hunt through the store for any of the extra stuff that the toy company sold for the dolls and find a few small things. Our next stop is the boutique that Claire loves. It is a cute little shop with some very pretty clothes. We are browsing through the dresses when I stop at an absolutely gorgeous pale pink one. I have nowhere to wear the dress and, of course, no money, but I can't seem to stop the impulse to pull it off the rack. The saleswoman walks up to me as I'm admiring it.

"That would look gorgeous on you. Let me check if we have one in a small enough size. She checks the other ones still on the rack and selects one.

"The smallest one we have is a size two, but it might work with some alterations. Why don't you try this one on?"

Claire is smiling at me and nods her head. I know I can't afford the dress, but why not try it on? So, I head to the dressing room and give it a go. A few moments later, I hear Claire calling out to me.

"Come out and show us."

I feel very unsure because the clerk was right; the dress is too big for me, but when have I ever been able to deny Claire anything?

"Oh, it is beautiful on you," the saleswoman says as she begins to fuss with the dress. "I'm sure our seamstress could make this a perfect fit for you."

"It is beautiful and I love it, but I have been sick for a while and now that I'm on the road to recovery, I'm hoping to get back to a healthy weight. It is probably best that I wait to buy it."

The saleswoman smiles at me and walks away as I head back to the dressing room. When I emerge, I'm back in my leggings and t-shirt and Claire is at the counter talking to the clerk and paying for a jacket. When she is done, we head back out into the sunshine and walk home to make some lunch. I haven't had this much fun in years and am feeling totally relaxed. Maybe that is what makes me brave enough to bring up my worries.

"Claire, are you upset that I have put you in danger? Or that my dad has made your home so secure?"

"What are you talking about? I love you and having you live with me is great. Mack has put us both in danger, not you. As for your dad's improvements, that is exactly what I think they are. Improvements. I was actually thinking of asking Abe if there is a way to update the camera system. So, tell me, where are these questions coming from?"

Another deep breath for me, since I brought up the topic, I need to see it through. "Yesterday, after my dad left, you seemed distracted all evening. I guess I just jumped to conclusions about why. Sorry."

"Don't apologize. I was distracted yesterday and I think we both need to work on being open with each other again. Let me tell you a story that Dawn told me yesterday."

39

Lazy Day

Sunday March 10, 2024
Claire

I roll over and turn off my alarm. I hardly slept last night, so despite being on call, I decide to sleep in. I really don't understand why I'm able to sleep fine when it is time to be awake and not at night when it's time to sleep. I know that one of the reasons I didn't sleep is the realization of what was tickling my brain yesterday. The very real possibility that Abe and Leon are the same person. How weird is it that I am dating a person who may be my stepmother's nephew and neither of them knows it?

I had sat in my bed using my laptop to find all that I could on Abe and his adoptive parents, Cheryl and Pete Carver. There wasn't much I didn't know; a high school graduation announcement for Abe from Douglass High School in Columbia, Missouri. He graduated from high school the year before I did. There is another announcement when he graduated from a community college with his associate's degree in digital forensic analysis.

There is little to nothing about his parents and, of course, the adoption would have been sealed, so I find no mention of that. I have already read all the articles on Eve's murder, but I read them again just to be sure I didn't miss anything. A search for other stories about women being killed by their husbands in Missouri twentyish years ago didn't result in anything. I'm left to wonder if Abe really is Leon or if it is just a strange coincidence. Bringing up questions to either Abe or Dawn would be awkward. I finally dozed off, trying to work out how to confirm or dismiss my theory.

I go back to sleep for another two hours and then get ready for the day. If I would have told my teenage self that sleeping until eight in the morning was sleeping in, she would laugh. But when you get up at five thirty daily, sleeping until eight feels like a real luxury. After getting ready for the day, I head to the kitchen for a cup of coffee. That is when I notice that Monica hasn't eaten any of the food in her dish. I know it is her food because Rachel is super picky and only eats canned food. Whereas Monica will eat whatever I feed her. Since Rachel also will gorge herself if there is food that she enjoys sitting out, I give Monica hard cat food only. She also never curled up on my bed last night.

I can see Lindsey through the front window, sitting out on the porch. She seems to be staring at her laptop. I wonder what she is looking at, so I head out there. She closes the lid of the laptop as I sit down and I ask her about Monica. I think the cat may have gotten out yesterday when Lindsey and her dad were working on the security upgrades. Lindsey hasn't seen Monica either, so I set food out on the porch before we head downtown to grab coffee.

The walk downtown feels like old times. I love the coffee and bookstore and am looking at cookbooks when I realize that I don't know where my friend is. I do a loop around the shop and spot her outside, just standing on the sidewalk. I set the cookbook down that I'm planning to buy and go out to join her. She is shaking, so I lead her to a bench and we both sit down. I talk her through a breathing exercise I learned in therapy and she tells me that she thought Mack was looking through the store window at her.

She has no proof of what she is saying, but I know it is important to support her in trusting her gut. Once she is calmer, we continue our browsing in other shops downtown. At an antique and vintage store, I stumbled across a doll that I coveted as a young girl. I remember the Christmas that both Lindsey and I were around eight years old and asked our parents for one of these dolls. The one I wanted had red hair and freckles, and the one Lindsey wanted had dark brown hair and brown eyes. The doll I'm holding is neither of those. She is the blond-haired, blue-eyed version, but there is just something about her that calls to me. As a child, I had no way of really understanding that the doll was very expensive, and I also didn't understand that my parents were likely already having issues. I decided right there and then that I was buying this doll and sharing her with Lindsey.

I show the doll to her and although she seems less excited than me about the find; we scour the store together for accessories. After I pay for my finds, we walk to this little boutique that I have come to love. The prices are high but the clothes are high end and they have a fabulous seamstress that makes clothes fit me just right. I see Lindsey holding a beautiful pink dress and talking to the store clerk. I approach the two of them and encourage her to try on the dress. When she comes out of the dressing room, she looks like a vision. I have no idea where she would wear a fancy dress, and I'm sure the price tag is high. As Lindsey changes out of the dress, I pay for the jacket that I found on the clearance rack and will wear to work. I ask the clerk to hold the dress for a few days and she tells me she can hold it for up to a week.

As we walk back home, I tell Lindsey the story of Dawn's sister Eve and we are both crying a little by the time we are on our block. But all that changes when we turn towards our house and see Monica curled up on a chair napping in the sun. Lindsey sprints up the stairs and gently picks up our wayward cat and cuddles her as I unlock the front door and turn the alarm to the at home setting. Looking at my friend contently stroking one of our cats, I think *things are all going to be okay. After all, we have been back a week and if Mack was going to do something, surely, he would have by now.*

40

The Dress

Sunday March 10, 2024
Mack

I'm just turning the corner when I spot Lindsey and Claire walking down the street the opposite way. They have their elbows linked together and look so much like little girls that I wonder if they are going to start skipping any minute now. I pull over and watch them until they are almost out of my sight. Then I drive a few blocks closer and continue this pattern until they walk into a coffee place. No doubt to buy some overpriced, high sugar, high calorie drinks. Lindsey had a serious addiction to those drinks when we first got together. I helped her to understand why drinking liquid calories was so bad for her. One mantra I had her repeat over and over was "Nothing tastes as good as thin feels". In the beginning, she was so easy to mold and shape that I had such high hopes for her. Now look at her, a few days back with her supposed friend, Claire, and she is back to her bad habits.

There is a municipal parking lot that employees of downtown businesses use, so I decided that is the best place to park the van. I walk by the coffee shop and see they sell books, too. No wonder Lindsey wanted to come here. She loves to have her nose buried in a book. I continue walking down the block and then loop around again. This time, I stop at the window and try to spot Lindsey. Sure enough, there she is, standing by a shelf, reading a book like she doesn't have a care in the world. Little does she know that her time away from me is quickly coming to an end. I see the moment Lindsey realizes I am staring at her. Her body goes rigid, and she looks around the entire store before glancing at the window. By the time she can fully focus on the window, I am opening the door to the cigar shop next door. Now this is a place that I could learn to love.

I buy a cigar based on the clerk's recommendation, then sit down on one of the comfortable leather recliners by this store's front window. As long as Lindsey and Claire walk this way, I will have a clear view of them when they pass. I'm betting on them coming this way because the other direction was the one they walked to get to the coffee place. Sure enough, a few moments later, they stroll by. I extinguish my cigar, cut the end and wrap it, then head out to continue my reconnaissance. The girls are so wrapped up in their conversation and looking in stores that neither ever even turns around. They spend an inordinate amount of time in one of those stores that the sign says is a vintage shop but really should say junk other people didn't want shop.

As they walk out, I see that Claire has a large bag of some junk she bought and both of them are laughing and smiling. They next go into a nice-looking women's clothing store. I look in and see them browsing through clothes, so I make a loop around the block. The next time I pass by, Lindsey is stepping out of a dressing room looking like a vision in a whitish pink dress. It is too big for her, but I'm sure it can be sewn or whatever to make it fit better. I hope she buys it. I duck into the doorway of an empty shop two doors down and wait. They must have turned the other way because I hear Lindsey's voice float towards me.

"Thanks for suggesting all this. It has been a great day. I'm sorry for my little freak out before. What are you making us for lunch?"

I can't hear Claire's reply, but I look out and see them walking away. Lindsey is still not carrying any bags. She must not have bought the dress. I sprint back to the van and follow the girl's home. After I watch them walk inside the house, I turn around and head back downtown. Walking into the boutique, the girls had left a while ago; I go straight to the clerk.

"Hi. My fiancé and her friend were in here recently, and she fell in love with a dress. Would you be able to help me figure out which one so I can buy it?"

"Wow, that was quick."

"Excuse me?"

"Claire had me hold the dress and said she would come back or send someone to buy it in the next few days. And here you are, not even an hour later."

"Yeah, well, Lindsey loved that dress. I think she wants to wear it to a wedding this summer."

"Umm, that's probably not the best idea."

"Why not?"

"Well, because it is so close to being white and women are not supposed to wear white to someone else's wedding."

This conversation is boring me. I just want to buy the dress and leave. "Okay, whatever. How much do I owe you for the dress?" I almost gasp when she says the total is over three hundred dollars. *What the hell kind of dress is this?* But I paid for it because after all I wasn't lying about the wedding this summer. I just hadn't told the clerk that it was Lindsey and my wedding, that she would be wearing it to. Either that or she can be buried in it.

41

Turning Plans into Action

Monday March 11, 2024

Mack

Last night, I told my mom and Brock that Lindsey and I were heading home in the morning. I could hardly sleep last night thinking about getting her back. Before either mom or Brock got home yesterday, I packed the van with everything except my cash and go bags. Now, I take everything out of the go bag and lay it on the bed just to be sure I haven't forgotten anything. A notebook, pen, keys to the lock on the cellar door, my dad's old gun, a box of ammo, some zip ties, and gloves. I haven't loaded the gun because I have no intention of shooting Lindsey, but I do want to scare her. I take the envelope I prepared for ma out of the bottom of the bag. It has a note telling her how much she means to me and that I won't be able to come back or contact her anytime soon. There is twenty thousand in cash in there which I hope ma never tells Brock about. I love my brother, but he is a leech like my dad. I take the envelope into ma's bathroom and put it below the foot soaker she uses every afternoon after work. I'm sure she will find it.

I have planned this day down to the very minute, and it is time to go. All the watching and waiting has made it clear that today is the day to strike. Claire works ten days on, so she has three more days to go in this rotation. Her schedule thus far has been very set, leaving each morning at twenty to seven and returning about three thirty. She occasionally goes out for dinner or runs to errands but is never gone long. Additionally, Lindsey's dad is on duty today but will be off the two days after that. He will be gone for about the same time frame as Claire. The change of shift at the police station is the best time to commit any crime. The patrol cars and the dumb asses who sit behind their wheels are all at the station until at least seven thirty, so their response time is much slower than usual. Her mom never comes over before nine in the morning, so my strike zone is seven to seven thirty.

I need to be back in the van with my cargo secured and heading out of town by seven thirty. The only thing I didn't plan on was the thunderstorm that is brewing, but that just seems fitting for Lindsey and my final departure from Springfield. The drive over to pick up Lindsey is uneventful, and I arrive at seven on the dot. After jamming the cameras and alarm system, I pull into the driveway parking right next to the cellar door. I slip on a pair of gloves and head on in. It takes me no time at all to open that door, walk through the basement, and run up the stairs. I stop at the top of the stairs and take a few deep breaths. Not because I'm nervous or out of shape, but because I'm so excited I need to slow down and do this right.

Lindsey has always been a deep sleeper, so it doesn't surprise me in the least that she never stirs as I enter her room. I take out the notebook and pen, placing them on the top of the dresser and open it to the page I have written the note on. I won't be leaving this note; no this is for Lindsey to copy on the next page in her own handwriting. I grab the nanny cam bear and shove it in my bag, then walk over to

Lindsey. It is unbelievably tempting to get undressed and slide into bed with her, but all that will have to wait. Instead, I lean down and whisper in her ear, "Time to wake up, sleeping beauty. We are heading home."

She sits up so quickly that our heads come close to colliding and starts to let out a scream. I slam my hand against her mouth, "None of that BS. Be a good little girl and get up."

Lindsey slides to the edge of the bed and stands. I grab one of her arms and steer her over to the dresser. "Now you are going to write your meddling friend Claire a little goodbye note. Don't worry, I already wrote it out for you so all you have to do is copy it and no funny business, write it exactly like I did." Lindsey is staring down at the note I wrote so I hand her the pen and read out loud while she writes.

"Claire, I'm heading home with Mack. I'm sorry for the trouble I caused and the lies I told you. Mack and I are soul mates, and so we are meant to be together. Please don't bother us, as I know you don't approve. Lindsey."

After I finish reading, I look over at what Lindsey wrote. Her hand was obviously shaking while she wrote it, but until the end she wrote my words exactly.

"Why did you add Best Friends since kindergarten?" I ask her, feeling the rage beginning to bubble up.

Lindsey looks up at me with that deer in the headlights look that she gets whenever I catch her, not following directions.

"That is the way we have signed all our notes since middle school. I thought it would make the note more believable."

It actually makes sense since chicks are always writing weird things to each other like that whole BFF thing, so I nod and pick up the note.

"Okay, fine. Now make the bed and then it's time to head home. Don't worry, we will talk about this little stunt you and Claire pulled on our way home and figure out how you are going to make it up to me."

After she complies with my direction to make the bed, Lindsey asks in a shaky voice; "Mack, can I please go to the bathroom and brush my teeth before we leave?"

Since everything has gone smoothly so far, we can spare a few minutes and hopefully letting her do this will get Lindsey to walk out of the house with me without causing issues.

"Yes, of course, sweetheart." I tell her as I guide her into the bathroom. She does her business quickly and we are leaving the bathroom when she takes off running. Of course, she can't outrun me and she screams as I encircle her waist. I lift her off the ground and pull her hard against my body. "And here I thought you loved me and were happy to see me. I was so hopeful we were going to do this the easy way." I quickly zip tie her hands behind her back then lower my mouth to the side of her neck and bite. The taste of her, especially when she starts to bleed, fuels me to get a move on. I set her down, keeping one hand on her arm and say "Walk".

We walk into the kitchen and I pull the note out of my pocket and set it on the table. As I open the basement door, Lindsey whimpers and tries to pull away again. We don't have time for this, so I let go of her arm and slam my fist into her temple. She crumples like a paper doll and I throw her over my shoulder. I really hoped that I had trained her well enough that she would not resist leaving, but I should've known better, seeing as we were standing in Claire's kitchen.

I am pissed as I stomp down the basement stairs and that is only made worse when I see that the door to outside is shut. The wind must have blown it closed while I was retrieving Lindsey. I push on it with my one free hand, but it will not open that easily, so I have to put Lindsey down. In my anger, I drop her more than set her down and her head hits the concrete. I think, *oh well, that's what she gets for putting up a fight*, as I turn back towards the door.

42

Forgotten Phon

Monday March 11, 2024
Claire

The wind has really picked up as I park my SUV in the usual spot at work and start walking in. As I cross the parking lot, I see the rest of my team heading towards one of the department CSI vans. I run to catch up with them and when I do, I ask breathlessly, "What is going on?"

Cal turns and says, "Why haven't you been answering your calls or text messages?"

That is the moment it hits me; my phone is still plugged in to the charger on my nightstand at home.

"OMG. I forgot my phone at home. Sorry. So where are we headed?"

"A possible crime scene. It sounds a lot like the two we had last week. An elderly lady was found dead in her bed," Cal tells me.

"Where is it at? I'll have us swing by my house and grab my phone if it isn't out of the way."

After I get the details on where my team has been called to, I know it is slightly out of the way to stop at my house, so I tell them I will drive myself to grab my phone, then meet them over there.

I pull up in front of my house and run up to the front door. After unlocking and opening the door, I go to turn the alarm off. *Wait, it is already off.* I am sure I rearmed it when I left this morning. Maybe Lindsey left and forgot to rearm it, but that seems unlikely.

"Hey Lindsey, where are you at?"

My question is met with complete silence. I walk down the hall to grab my phone and check if Lindsey is sleeping. I peek into her room and see she is not there. My room is empty too, as are the office and bathroom. The panic is rising in me so much that I forget to grab my cell phone. I walk by the family room on my way to the kitchen, calling out for Lindsey again, but she isn't answering me. As I turn into the kitchen, I notice that the basement door isn't all the way closed, and the light over the stairs is on. My heart is beating in my ears as I stare at that door.

Lindsey hasn't gone down to the basement since she got back here. I know that Mack used to keep her chained in the basement of the house that they rented in Denver. If she is down there, something isn't right. I open the door the rest of the way and call down for her. There is no response. I guess it is possible that I left the light on and one of the cats pushed the door open. I walk down a few stairs and reach to pull the string to turn off the light when I see Lindsey on the floor with blood pooling around her head. I run down the rest of the stairs and towards Lindsey. I never see Mack or his punch coming, but I feel it.

I fall to the ground with my jaw and head ringing. Mack drags me by my feet towards the under-stairs crawl space. I press my eyes closed, hoping he will believe I am unconscious. He kicks me hard, but I don't flinch. I hear him turn and stomp away. I ease my eyes open just slightly and see Mack pick up Lindsey. He throws her unconscious, bleeding body over his shoulder and begins stomping up the stairs.

I turn my head slightly and see the garden shovel. I have to stop him because I know that Lindsey was right. Mack will kill her this time!

43

Delusions of Victory

Monday March 11, 2024

Mack

I have both hands pushing on the cellar doors when I hear her voice. *Claire! What the hell is she doing here?* I move quickly to be in the darkest area of the basement off to the right of the stairs and pounce as soon as she runs towards Lindsey. A hard punch delivered to the left side of her face sends her sprawling out on the floor. I pull her by the feet out of the way of the stairs and kick her once, just for good measure. She is out cold.

With Lindsey over my shoulder, I start towards the staircase and shoot a glance over to where Claire lays unconscious on the floor. I wonder, *what did that wisp of a girl think she was going to do? Save Lindsey? Goes to show how dumb she is.* If I had more time, I would take care of her once and for all, but I know that my window of opportunity to get Lindsey out of here free and clear is closing quickly. So, I leave her to live with the knowledge that she failed her supposed best friend.

I take my anger out on the stairs by stomping as hard as I can. I know I need to release it so I can be fully in control and not make mistakes. Despite this morning not going exactly as I had hoped, I'm confident that victory is mine. Claire is unconscious, I have Lindsey, and, in a few minutes, we will be on our way home.

The stair beneath me gives way just as I crunch my boot onto it. I feel the breaking and my feet going through the wood. *Shit!* Lindsey flies out of my arms and halfway through the open door above us. She isn't moving at all. If she is dead, I'm just going to leave her body here when I get loose. Both my legs are dangling beneath the stair tread and pain is shooting up my right one. I grasp the open tread of the stair above me and begin to lift myself up. Pulling to free my feet. Just as my left foot begins lifting out, I hear a whoosh and then feel a shattering crack upside my head. A pain reverberates through me and I lift my hands to try to turn to see what is happening when the next blow hits. I pitch forward again, feeling blood pouring down the side of my head.

As I'm pulling myself back up, I scream "What the F…"

44

Doctors, Lawyers and Cops;
Oh my!

Monday March 11, 2024
Claire

When I regain consciousness, it's clear that I'm in a hospital room. I look around and see my dad and Dawn sitting in chairs by a window.

"Hey, look who's back with us. How are you feeling?" My dad asks as he walks up to the side of my bed and takes my hand in his.

"My head hurts and I'm not sure how I got here?"

"The doctor tells us that you have a concussion and most likely lost consciousness after a burst of adrenaline wore off. How much do you remember?"

I'm trying to form my thoughts to answer him, when my dad continues.

"Actually no, don't tell us. The police are waiting to talk to you and it's probably best that you tell them first. I've called an attorney and he will come over and be here when the police question you."

"Dad, is that really necessary?"

"Claire, you know I have had my own issues with the Springfield police department and the way they conduct investigations, so yes, it is necessary."

I know he is right, but I work for the department and I know what I did. I can't see how anyone could argue that what I did wasn't self-defense.

"I understand what you're saying and will have the lawyer with me when I talk to the detectives. Do you know how Lindsey is?"

Dawn walks up and takes my dad's free hand in hers. He shakes his head and replies, "We really don't have any information on her. Sorry, sweetie. Let me call Mike Davidson and let him know you're awake."

As my dad makes his call, I press the call button for a nurse and when she arrives, ask for pain medication. She returns with two pills and tells Dawn and me that the doctor will be by soon to examine me. As if she has conjured him up, the door opens and in walks a doctor. After introductions, he examines me and asks a bunch of questions that I think are supposed to tell him if I am having brain issues.

"You are doing remarkably well, considering all you have been through. You do have a concussion, so I would like to keep you overnight for observation and if there are no issues, we will get you home in the morning. How does that sound?"

"Sounds good to me."

"I will have the nurse make sure you get a dinner tray. Do you have questions?"

"Do you know anything about my friend Lindsey Peterson?"

The look on his face is so sad that I just know she is dead. "I'm truly sorry. I can't discuss another patient with you."

After the doctor leaves the room, Dawn sits back down by my bed. "Your friend Abe stopped by. He seems nice. He asked that we call him when you wake up. Do you want me to do that, or do you want to wait a bit?"

I'm startled that Dawn met Abe. "How long was he here? Did you talk to him?"

Dawn smiles, "Just for ten minutes and don't worry, I didn't let your dad give him the third degree."

I have so many questions, but whatever the medication was that the nurse gave me is making my brain fuzzy. I drift back to sleep and dream about Lindsey. I startle awake when I feel a hand gently touch my shoulder.

"Claire," my dad is saying softly.

I open my eyes and reply, "I'm awake."

"Claire, this is Mike Davidson. He will be your attorney. Dawn and I are going to go get a cup of coffee while the two of you talk. Do you need anything while we're out?"

"Are you going to Starbucks?" I ask hopefully.

I hear Dawn chuckle and my dad replies, "We weren't planning to, but we will if that is what you want."

"Yes, please. My usual would be great."

My dad nods and I hear Dawn ask him as they are leaving my hospital room, "You know her usual drink from Starbucks?" The rest of their conversation is cut off as the door closes.

I turn my head and see that the attorney is now sitting next to my bed. Using the control buttons, I put the bed and myself into a seated position just as he launches into his legal spiel.

"As your dad stated, I am Mike Davidson, and he has retained me to be your attorney. Your dad didn't tell me much about what was going on, so I would like you to start as far back as you think I need to know and tell me why the police want to question you."

After about forty minutes of talking, Mike goes to get the detectives while I head to the bathroom to freshen up. I'm shocked by what I see in the mirror. I have a black eye, a goose egg size bump on the side of my head and although I'm always pale, it is worse than ever. My skin could be described as ghostly and almost translucent. My hands are shaking as I gently touch the side of my head before heading back to my hospital bed.

The door to my hospital room opens and I watch as Mike David-son, Detective Kass Minor, Detective Nichols, and two men in suits walk in. I know they have questions, but so do I. Mike has told me that they will probably not be willing to answer my questions, but I still intend to ask them. He also told me that I am not to answer any of their questions until he tells me to.

"Claire, the doctors tell us you are going to be alright. That is such a relief. If you're up to it, we have questions. You know my partner, Detective Nichols, and this is Detective Mills with the state police and Cliff Triton, an investigator in the internal affairs division." She says as she points to each of the men who accompanied her into my room. "Detective Mills and IA Triton are here to oversee this investigation and be sure that I'm not giving you any preferential treatment. We would like to ask you some questions about what happened at your house earlier today," Detective Minor says as she sits by my bedside.

"I will answer your questions the best I can, but first I need to know if Lindsey is alive?"

45

We Regret to Inform You

Monday March 11, 2024

Brock

I'm sitting in my room playing Madden 25, when I hear two car doors slam. Looking out my window, I see what has to be detectives heading to the front door of the trailer. Immediately I think, *oh shit, I'm going back to prison.* I should have left with Mack this morning when he headed back to Colorado, but it's not like he asked me to join him and I've had a pretty good thing going here the past few weeks.

When Bud first approached me with his idea for home invasions on people he did odd jobs for, I thought, *this is just like what my dad was doing when he got sent up to Jefferson City Maximum Security Prison for the rest of his life.* Bud told me he only wanted me to drive the getaway car. He said he knew when these people were home and which ones had cash in their houses and that I'd be shocked how much cash some of the old people just keep lying around. I turned him down the first time he asked, but then I couldn't get anyone to hire me, so the next time he came around I agreed.

So far, we have done six jobs together, and each one went off with no signs of trouble. I'm replaying the jobs in my head when I hear my ma open the front door and then scream. Without even really thinking about it, I race out to the living room to see what's the matter. Ma is sitting on the couch sobbing and the detectives are just standing there, so I've got no choice but to talk to them.

"What's going on? What did you say to my mom?"

The female detective responds, "We are here to let you know that Mack Tiswell is dead."

"What the hell happened?" I was not prepared for her response.

"He was killed during the commission of a crime. That is all we are at liberty to say at this point."

Mack killed while committing a crime. It just didn't fit. Oh, wait, unless it had something to do with Lindsey. I notice the other detective is holding out a piece of paper towards me.

Taking the paper, I hear him say, "This is the information on contacting the medical examiner's office and the case number pertaining to your brother's case. We do have some questions, but can come back in a few days when your mother has had time to calm down."

Ma shrieks from the couch, "CALM DOWN. How the hell do you think I'm ever going to calm down? My Mack is dead and you are accusing him of being a criminal. Just ask your damn questions and leave."

I sit down next to her and turn back to the detectives, waving my arm for them to sit down. Once they take a seat and take out their little notebooks, it is the female detective who starts talking again.

"We are sorry for your loss. As I told you, Mrs. Tiswell, when we first arrived, I'm Detective Kass Minor, and this is my partner, Detective Dave Nichols. It is our understanding that Mack lives in Colorado. Is that correct?"

Both ma and I nod and I notice that neither of us verbally answers the question. The nodding seems good enough for the detective as she continues her questions.

"What was the nature of his being back in Springfield, Missouri?"

Ma looks at her like she is some kind of idiot and says, "Visiting his family. Why is that a crime now, too?"

"No, ma'am, no crime in that. What is your understanding of his relationship with Lindsey Peterson?"

Yep, I was right, this crime Mack supposedly committed involved her. I would bet money that her dad is the one who killed my brother and he will get away scot-free.

"They have been dating for years and live together in Denver. They are here to visit their families together, but Lindsey hasn't graced us with her presence." Ma tells the detectives. She is still crying and takes a second to blow her nose before continuing. "Does Mack being dead have something to do with her?"

"We are not at liberty to discuss that. I only have one more question then we will go. "Do either of you know why Mack would have almost seventy-five thousand dollars in cash in a duffle bag in his van?"

What! What, the What! My brain comes to a screeching halt. Mack had that much money and he was letting ma and me barely scrape by. Plus, he made me pay him for his old truck.

It is ma who answers them, "We never heard about, nor saw any money. Isn't that right, Brock?"

"I sure as hell didn't know Mack had that kind of cash. Shit, I wouldn't have bought that bucket of chicken if I knew he was loaded. We could've had a nice steak dinner." Ma smacks my arm hard. "Ow, What?"

Ma is shaking her head and staring me down, "Your brother is dead and you're talking about paying for a ten-dollar bucket of chicken."

"More like twenty bucks, but yeah, I get it." The detectives are standing to leave when I say, "I have a question. When can we pick up Mack's van and all this cash you said was his?"

Both detectives continue walking towards the door. The man detective says, "We'll let you know," and they both leave. I say to ma, "You know they are never going to give us that money, right?"

She smacks me again before getting up and going into her room.

46

The Truck

Monday March 11, 2024
Detective Kass Minor

As we walk out of the Tiswell's place after notifying them of Mack's death, I stare at the black truck with Colorado plates parked there.

"Hey, Nichols. You remember the scene we were at when the call came in for this case?"

"Yeah, not much of a scene. I have a feeling the ME is going to rule Pearl Harris' death to be from natural causes. Why?"

"I told you that two separate neighbors told me that there were two men mowing Mrs. Haris' lawn yesterday morning. They also said that despite the fact that Pearl walked around the block every day at six o'clock that they had not seen her that evening. So, it is likely that Pearl was already dead before then. One of those neighbors, the one who discovered her body and called it in, went over there at six this morning to have her regular morning coffee with Pearl.

"Okay, makes sense, but where are you going with this?"

Dave Nichols is not the worst partner I've ever had, but he is certainly not the best either. I miss the days of working with Mitch Leet. Mitch never phoned it in. He treated every case we worked with the same dogged preciseness. No, with Nichols, the magnitude of the case is directly in line with how much effort he puts in.

"The thing is, both witnesses described the lawn guys having a black truck with out-of-state plates. Neither had ever seen the truck in the neighborhood before. So, look at that truck. It matches their descriptions. Want to bet that truck belongs to Mack Tiswell?"

"Are you suggesting that in the week Tiswell was back in town, he had time to start a lawn crew and that somehow Mrs. Harris' death is not from natural causes?"

I want to sigh, but I suppress it. Instead, I respond, "I find it odd that in the time that Mack Tiswell has been back in Springfield, we have had three unattended deaths of elderly citizens. Add in that Mack had seventy-five grand in cash in a duffle bag."

"Three?"

"Yeah, Burgeon has an open case of an elderly woman found dead in her recliner. Plus, Hazel Green and Pearl Harris make three."

"Didn't the ME already declare Hazel Green's death to be from natural causes?"

Again, I have to suppress a sigh; I mean, I'm basically laying out that Mack Tiswell is a serial killer and Nichols is worried about the ME's ruling.

"I'm going to run it by the captain and see what he has to say."

"You do that, Minor,"

47

Hospital Time

Tuesday March 12, 2024
Claire

The doctor came by early this morning and told me that I would be discharged today. I called my dad right after the doctor left the room, so he and Dawn have been sitting here for hours. They stopped by my house before coming here and brought me clean clothes since the ones I was wearing yesterday are in an evidence bag at the police station. I have been sitting here fully dressed, waiting since I got my stuff. I want to go see Lindsey.

Her mom and dad stopped by yesterday and told me that Lindsey was alive but in a coma. She is in rough shape with swelling and bleeding in her brain. Her dad thanked me for what he called "once again saving his little girl's life" and then chastised me for putting myself in harm's way again.

I wasn't sure what he thought I should have done differently, but in retrospect, I at least should have had my phone on me when I went into the basement.

"What is taking so long?" I whine to no one in particular.

Dawn looks up from the game she is playing on her phone. "Claire, you are on hospital time, not regular time."

"What does that mean?"

Dawn comes and sits beside my bed, "When my mom was in and out of the hospital while she battled cancer, my family learned that hospitals run at their own pace. We called it hospital time. The staff in hospitals do things in order of priority, not based on who was first. So, if they have a lot going on this morning, printing your discharge and getting you out of here may not be a top priority. But I will go check what is going on."

My dad chuckles as Dawn walks out of the room. "Well, Claire Bear, if anyone can get you out of here, it is Dawn. She is a force of nature. So, tell me about Abe."

I groan and roll my eyes. Abe stopped by to check on me just before dad and Dawn got here this morning and was here when they walked in. His timing couldn't have been worse because I know him visiting again peaked my dad's interest.

"Abe and I have been casually dating for a few months. He also works at the department but he is in the cyber investigations division. He likes fried chicken, freezing cold Cokes with lots of crushed ice, has never seen the ocean, and is a Sagittarius. What else would you like to know?"

My dad is laughing when he responds, "Alright smart ass. I get it. You don't want to talk about your love life with dear old dad. But when you're ready, you should bring him to dinner with Dawn and me."

Dawn walks back with a bedraggled-looking nurse right behind her. The nurse looks at the identification bracelet on my wrist and says, "Let's get you out of here." She then hands me a stack of papers about concussion recovery and tells me that she will have a CNA with a wheelchair come by soon so they can to wheel me out. "So, mom and dad, you are welcome to go pull the car up and Claire will be right out," she says.

My dad is about to correct her when I interrupt, "I'm not ready to leave the hospital."

The nurse now looks confused, "I'm sorry, what? Your mom came and got me to speed up your discharge and now you're saying you're not ready to leave."

"Oh, I'm ready to be discharged, but they don't need to get the car because I'm going to check on my friend Lindsey. And by the way, Dawn isn't my mom."

"Fine, I will have the CNA wheel you off the floor, then you can make your way to the ICU. But I'm not sure if you will get into your friend's room because that floor has very strict visiting rules."

The nurse walks out and I turn to Dawn and my dad, "I'd like to see someone stop me from checking on Lindsey."

48

Self-Defense

Wednesday March 13, 2024
Lindsey

Where am I? Why is it so dark? As the room comes into focus, I re-alize that I am laying in a bed in a hospital. Slowly turning my head because it hurts so badly, I see Claire sleeping in a chair next to my bed. She has a black eye and a large bump on her head. Now I am wondering *what the hell happened?* I wish my head would stop throbbing so I could think. Hitting the button, I try to ease the bed up to sitting, but it hurts and I let out a groan.

Claire sits up and looks over at me. "Thank God. You are awake. We have all been so worried about you?"

Through dry, chapped lips I hear my voice come out as a squeak. "What happened?"

"Two days ago, Mack broke into our house. I came home from work because I forgot my cell phone and found the alarm turned off. I knew you would never leave it like that."

"He hurt you too, didn't he?"

"Yes, he did, but it's okay because he is dead."

"What?"

"When I found you in the basement, there was so much blood, I freaked out and ran down the stairs. That is when Mack came at me. He punched me in the face; I fell and hit my head. I laid on the ground, pretending to be out cold because I remembered you telling me that you did that when he was beating you."

"When did I tell you that?"

"That isn't important right now. Anyway, Mack pulled me out of the way, picked you up, and started up the stairs. But you know that one stair is bad and we both avoid stepping on it. Well, Mack didn't know that and it broke when he stomped on it on the way up. His legs went through the wood, he pitched forward, and you flew out of his grip. I ran up behind him and hit him in the head with a garden shovel."

"That killed him?"

"Well, I hit him a lot, so yeah, it did. After I hit him, I tried to get past the two of you to go for help, but I passed out. The doctors tell me that I had a massive surge of adrenaline and when it wore off, my body collapsed. What I now know is that after about an hour, when I hadn't shown up to the crime scene my team was headed to, Cal came over to the house.

He found my SUV parked on the street, and despite the thunderstorm that was raging, the front door of the house was wide open, so he knew something was wrong. He walked in and found you at the top of the basement stairs, unconscious and bleeding. That is when he called 911. Luckily, there was a cruiser only two blocks away, so they arrived quickly. When the police arrived, we were both unconscious and Mack was dead.

You have been unconscious since then and the doctors have been worried about the swelling and possible bleeding in your brain. I'm so relieved you're awake because they were going to do brain surgery tomorrow morning to relieve the pressure if you hadn't regained consciousness. The detectives will probably want to talk to you soon."

"Why? Are they charging you for killing him?"

"I don't think so. Detective Minor told me it sounds like a straightforward case of self-defense. I was defending both of us against deadly force. I think they want to talk to you to figure out what happened in the time I left for work and came back to find you and Mack in the basement. You wrote a note saying you were leaving with him."

"I don't remember any of that."

"That's okay. I figured out that Mack made you write it when the detectives showed me the note and I saw the Best Friends since Kindergarten line. I knew that was you sending me a coded message, and I told them that. You aren't in any trouble. I'm not sure how, but the detectives told me that they already knew Mack forced you to write that note. I'm going to go tell the nurses that you are awake so they can call the doctor. Then I'll call your parents. I sent them home this morning to shower and change. They are going to be over the moon to see you up."

I smile at my best friend and think of all the things I have to thank her for. "Claire, I'll never be able to repay you for saving me, but please never hesitate to ask me for anything."

49

Starting Over

Lindsey
Monday April 8, 2024

I spent three weeks in the hospital and know I'm lucky to be alive. Today is my first day working for Dawn and her brother Gary at their auto shop. When I went to talk to Dawn about it last week and she offered me the job, I told her I couldn't be there right when they opened because of the bus schedule. She told me they had a car that they had fixed up and were selling that I could buy on payments from them. It is 2008 Volkswagen Jetta and even though it is not in the best body shape; it runs great. I have so much to be grateful for, but I'm also anxious about Claire.

She hasn't been back to work since that day Mack broke in and tried to kidnap me. I know she is struggling with having killed him, but all I feel is relief. I would never have been safe as long as Mack was alive. I have no memory of that day or the first week I was in the hospital. My neurologist says that it is perfectly normal for someone with a head injury to have memory loss. He said that I have a Traumatic Brain Injury and that it is entirely possible that I will never regain those memories. I'm okay with that because all the details I have been told sound like a living nightmare.

My dad, Claire, and Detective Minor have all shared pieces of that day with me, so I have a pretty good idea of what happened. Because my dad is a police officer, he knows more than most people would be able to find out. Things like the fact that Mack had bought a van and welded a dog cage into the back. Presumably that was where he planned to put me when we left town. Or the fact that Mack had a lot of cash in the van and that Detective Minor is looking into his connection to a string of home invasion robberies. I'm not sure I believe that Mack was robbing people when he came back to Springfield, but I'll leave the sleuthing up to the detectives.

I do believe that Mack was stalking me the entire time I was back in Springfield and that he had been in the house at least twice before he grabbed me. My dad told me that they found a teddy bear that was a nanny cam in his bag and an app on his phone with saved footage of me sleeping. Based on everything that was found out after Mack died, there is no doubt that what Claire did was justified. The thing is that my best friend wasn't made to take another person's life no matter the circumstance. No, she is too kindhearted for what she had to do and I can see that it is crushing her. I talked with my dad about it and he told me he has seen it in cops who have justifiably shot someone in the line of duty. He assured me that most of them just need time and counseling to move beyond it. What worries me is that he said most of them. When I asked him about those who that doesn't work for, he shook his head and had the saddest expression.

I mailed a letter to Emma Jean this weekend to thank her for helping Claire and ask her to let our landlords know that we will not be returning. I can't even begin to think about facing that house in Denver. I let her know that Mack is dead and that I am moving on with my life. I'm not sure if I'll ever hear back from her, but I know that she and Mr. Harris are a big part of why I'm alive today. My dad asked me if I want to be named in the probate case regarding Mack's assets and I said no. His mom can have whatever there is because as far as I'm concerned, I want to close that chapter of my life and never look back.

50

Aftershocks

Claire

Monday April 8, 2024

It has been six weeks since that fateful day that Mack tried to kidnap Lindsey and I killed him. I haven't been back to work. The first two weeks, I was on administrative leave while my role in Mack's death was investigated. After I was completely cleared of any wrong-doing, my leave turned into medical for two more weeks. I was still having daily headaches, and my doctor refused to clear me to return to work. When he was willing to clear me medically, I told him about my not sleeping, the nightmares, shaking and uncontrollable crying. He put me on leave for the indefinite future and referred me to a psychiatrist and a counselor that specializes in PTSD.

I have been seeing both of them and now I understand that I am struggling with having broken one of my own moral beliefs. I feel like I crossed a line into evil, so even though I know that Mack would have killed Lindsey and possibly me that day, I'm struggling with having taken his life. I replay that day over and over in my head, trying to figure out if the outcome could have been different. *What if I had re-*

membered to grab my cell phone and dialed 911 instead of attacking Mack? What if I had only hit him once or twice? What if I had taken Lindsey more seriously and made sure she was never alone?

The what if thinking is what makes it so hard to sleep. I did this a lot when my mom disappeared and learned in therapy then that I need to recognize and challenge these thoughts. That was easier to do when I wasn't the one who took another person's life. I wanted to go to Mack's funeral, but my lawyer, dad and Dawn, all told me that I shouldn't. I logically know they were right, but I feel like I need closure and forgiveness. Not that his mother and brother are likely to ever forgive me.

Since that day, my dad and Mr. Peterson enclosed the back deck and built a really nice laundry room in there. They replaced the outside cellar door with a much more secure and modern one, fixed the broken step, as well as adding a switch at the top of the basement stairs that now turns on all the basement lights at once. Not that I have been down there. I'm not sure when I will be ready to face the basement. My counselor says that I don't need to even begin to think about confronting that fear. I have much more pressing things to worry about.

Abe stops by every day after work and we sit and chat. He redid the security and camera systems so they are hard wired and much less vulnerable to hacking. In order to avoid the subject of my issues, I asked him to tell me more about his birth parents. Turns out I was wrong; Abe is not Leon. Abe was born in St. Louis and his mom and dad were never married and his dad is serving life in prison at the Jefferson State Prison. Abe told me that no extended family could be located, so he went into the system. The Carvers were his one and only foster family, and they adopted him as soon as they could. He actually finds it intriguing that Dawn had a similar incident in her family and thinks we should ask her more about Leon. I'm not sure that I want to pick at that emotional scab.

I'm sitting on the front porch when Lindsey comes out. She looks better every day and today she is going to work at Dawn's shop for the first time. Dawn sold her a car on payments and Lindsey really seems to be looking forward to going to work.

"Have a good day at work." I say as she walks by me.

"Oh, sorry, I didn't even see you sitting there. I guess I'm too caught up in my own thoughts. How are you today?"

"No worries. I'm okay. So, are you looking forward to going to work?"

Lindsey smiles at me in such a genuine way that I'm overcome with happiness for her. "I really am. It has been so long since I acted like an adult that I'm ready for all the parts of adulting. The good and the bad. The working, laundry, bills and shopping, hanging out with friends and fun times. How about you? When do you think you're going back to work?"

Now there is the million-dollar question to which I have no answer, so I just shrug.

Lindsey was in the hospital for two weeks after Mack attacked her and has no memory of that day. In a lot of ways, I think she is lucky not to. I have all kinds of memories of that day. The smell and feel of Mack's blood as it splattered on me, the screams I made as I hit him, the clunk of the shovel hitting his head, and the relief I felt when he stopped moving. All of it plays over and over in my head like a horror movie. I, Claire Learner, killed a man in my own home.